MOB TIES 4

**Lock Down Publications and Ca$h
Presents**

MOB TIES 4
A Novel by *SAYNOMORE*

Lock Down Publications
P.O. Box 944
Stockbridge, Ga 30281
www.lockdownpublications.com

Lock Down Publications
Like our page on Facebook: Lock Down Publications @
www.facebook.com/lockdownpublications.ldp

Book interior design by: **Shawn Walker**
Edited by: **Nuel Uyi**

Stay Connected with Us!

Text **LOCKDOWN** to 22828 to stay up-to-date with new releases, sneak peaks, contests and more…
Thank you!

Submission Guideline.

Submit the first three chapters of your completed manuscript to ldpsubmissions@gmail.com, subject line: Your book's title. The manuscript must be in a .doc file and sent as an attachment. Document should be in Times New Roman, double spaced and in size 12 font. Also, provide your synopsis and full contact information. If sending multiple submissions, they must each be in a separate email.

Have a story but no way to send it electronically? You can still submit to LDP/Ca$h Presents. Send in the first three chapters, written or typed, of your completed manuscript to:

LDP: Submissions Dept
P.O. Box 944
Stockbridge, Ga 30281

DO NOT send original manuscript. Must be a duplicate.

Provide your synopsis and a cover letter containing your full contact information.

Thanks for considering LDP and Ca$h Presents.

SAYNOMORE

Deoblow kneeled down as he said a prayer over his brother's grave. He placed two roses down on top of his grave, making an X. He kissed his two fingers, and touched his brother's headstone before getting up.

"Today makes two years my brother has been dead, and all I was told is that someone dropped a half-dead man off at his front gate with a damn bomb in him, killing him and his men."

"Mr. Deoblow, you been gone five years. A lot has taken place since your absence."

"Carlito, I'm back now and I want answers to my little brother's murder. I want to know who he was doing business with."

"Yes, Mr. Deoblow."

"But first, Carlito, let's go see Carlos, he's waiting on us," replied Deoblow.

Deoblow walked in the warehouse, surrounded by his men as he smoked his Cuban cigar, looking at Carlos hanging from the ceiling by chains from his hands that were tied together. Blood covered his whole body, dripping to the floor, as Deoblow walked up to him and blew smoke in his face. Carlos looked up at him.

"Carlos, it's been a long time since I saw you. I really wish it could have been under better circumstances face to face. Anyway, I'll get to the point. I want to know who killed my brother."

With a low tone and shortness of breath, Carlos said: "So you come to me, why?"

"Just to see if you heard something."

"I only know the story. I was surprised when I found out of his death," replied Carlos.

Shaking his head, with a sinister look in his eyes, Deoblow said: "I don't believe you at all. Take a look at these pictures of this girl. Do you know who she is?"

Carlos looked at the picture of Jamila that Deoblow was holding up in front of him. "I don't know her. I have never seen her before. Who is she?"

"I don't know yet. She pops up—a few months later— then my brother gets killed. I'm trying to find out who this mystery girl is. But you know what's funny? You told me you don't know who she is. But look at these pics. The photos are from a Camaro a few blocks up from my brother's house, and guess who is standing next to our mystery girl?"

Carlos looked at the picture of him and Jamila, then at Deoblow. Deoblow placed the pictures back in the top right pocket of his jacket, then grabbed the side of Carlos's face and rammed his knife in the side of his head. Carlos let out a scream, as blood came dripping from his head.

"Come on ya, let this piece of shit die slowly."

Deoblow and his men walked out the warehouse, leaving Carlos hanging dead from the chains.

Chapter 1

"Symone, I need you to drop off all the deposits at the bank today. Lorenzo has everything waiting on you now."

"Okay."

Symone hung up the phone as she was driving through the city with Slim Boogie.

"Slim, we got to go meet up with Lorenzo. Jamila has some deposits she needs me to take to the bank."

"Where is he at?" asked Slim.

"*Destiny's*, as always."

"Say less, we on our way there now."

***

Jamila walked to the sliding doors of her office, and was looking at the city when her phone went off. She walked back to her desk and picked up her phone.

"Hello."

"Hey, Jamila, it's Cello."

"Hey, Cello. How are you?"

"Not good. I'm calling to let you know that Felipe's brother is out of prison and he has been asking about you, and two weeks ago he killed Carlos."

"Oh my God, I'm sorry to hear that. What is his brother's name?" asked Jamila.

"Kenotea Deoblow. Jamila, be careful. He has no limits."

"I will. I'm sorry for your loss, Cello."

Jamila hung up the phone and sat down, placing her fingers on her head as she started to think.

***

Deoblow was looking at the picture of him and Felipe at the dog track six years ago. They took it right before he went to prison. Just then, as he was looking over his records in Felipe's office, Carlito walked up to him.

"Mr. Deoblow, we found out who our mystery girl is."

"So don't stand there looking at me, tell me who she is!" replied Deoblow.

Her name is Jamila LaCross. She is the head of the LaCross family in New York City, and she is the Queen Don. She is also the daughter of Anthony Catwell."

"Wait, Carlito," replied Deoblow, "you said she is Anthony Catwell's daughter?"

"Yes, sir."

"Now all the pieces are being put together. You know what? Let's pay this Mrs. LaCross a visit."

"Should I call and set it up?" asked Carlito.

"No, let's make it a surprise visit."

"Okay, I'm on it now, sir."

"Anthony Catwell's daughter came back and killed my brother over her father's killing. Now I know why she came down here!"

***

Jamila picked up the phone and called Lorenzo.

"Hello."

"Lorenzo, we need to talk as soon as possible."

"What's up?"

"Not over the phone, come to *Jelani's*," replied Jamila.

"I'll be there after Symone picks up these deposits."

"Okay, I'll be waiting on you."

Jamila hung up her phone. Afterwards, she went and got a bottle of Gray Goose from the bar in her office and sat it down on her desk. Once she sat down, she poured herself a shot and placed her hands on her head.

Chapter 2

Slim Boogie stopped at the red light as they were headed to *Destiny's*.

"Yo, Symone, look over there by the pizza joint. Ain't that Cam?"

Symone looked out the window of Slim Boogie's Hummer.

"Yea, that's his ass. He just don't know he is a dead man. He ran off with a hundred thousand dollars."

"Damn, I knew he ran off with some money, but I ain't know it was that much," replied Slim. "How did he get that much to run off with?"

"He was one of Jamila's runners," said Symone.

"Where is he walking to?"

"I don't know, but we are about to follow him, Slim Boogie."

When the light turned green, they followed him into one of the PJ's in Queens. Pulling up, Slim looked at him as he walked into the building. Stepping out the Hummer, Symone put her hoodie on because it was raining.

"So what you want to do?" asked Slim Boogie.

'You know how this is going to go, Slim, come on."

Once in the building, Symone looked down at the floor.

"Slim, I think he went in this door over here, look at the muddy footprints. Stop here."

Symone took her gun out as she knocked on the door.

"Who is it?" said the voice from the other side of the door.

"Meech."

When the door opened, Symone smacked the man in the face with the gun, dropping him. Cam came running to the door, and Symone pointed her gun at him.

"Where the fuck is my money at?" yelled Symone.

"Chill, chill, I got it right here in the back," replied Cam.

"Slim, don't let this nigga get up off the floor. Take me to my money before I unload this clip in your ass."

Symone followed Cam to the back room. He pulled a book bag from out the closet, and placed it on the bed.

"Open it up."

"Look, Symone, It's all here plus fifty thousand dollars."

"I see, zip it back up."

Once the book bag was closed, Cam threw it by her feet.

"We good, Symone?" asked Cam.

"Yea, we good."

Cam looked at Symone as she fired three rounds in his chest. She watched him fall to the floor. "You know the price of disloyalty is death. What's Red Invee's number one rule? *There are no second chances.*" Cam closed his eyes as Symone shot him in the face, taking his life. Slim Boogie looked at Symone coming out the room with the bag in her hand.

"Symone, I swear I ain't have anything to do with him taking the money."

"You are guilty by association."

Slim watched as she let two rounds fire into the nigga's head.

"Damn, Symone, low key."

"No witnesses, no case. I have no understanding for the bullshit. That nigga knew he was a dead man. Come on, let's get the fuck up out of here."

Once back in the Hummer, Symone called Lorenzo.

"Hey, Lorenzo, my bad. I know I'm late, but I ran into Cam."

"Where is he at?" asked Lorenzo.

"With the rest of the people who were disloyal to this family. I also picked that bread up from him."

"Good, how long before you get here?"

"Ten minutes at the most," replied Symone.

"I'll be here when you get here, and leave *that* at the front desk when you get here."

Okay, I will. Come on, Slim, let's hurry up and get there."

***

Lorenzo was sitting down eating when Symone walked in. Wearing Timberland boots, she had on some yellow sweatpants, and a yellow t-shirt with a white NBA logo on it. When Lorenzo saw her, he pointed down at her left boot. Symone looked down to see blood on her boot. She took a napkin off the table and wiped her boot off.

"You need to be more careful, Symone—The right cop could have questioned you about that," said Lorenzo.

"I will be more careful. How you doing today?" asked Symone.

"Good. Listen, to me, there is a guy over there in a blue sports jacket. Don't look at him. Go to the bathroom and then come back out and look at him. I'm going to the bar, so meet me over there."

Lorenzo sat down at the bar, and watched Symone go to the bathroom. "Bartender, let me get two shots of Vodka."

"Coming right up."

When Symone came out the bathroom, she looked at the man Lorenzo told her about. Symone walked to the bar and sat down next to Lorenzo.

"Did you see him?" asked Lorenzo.

"Yea, who is he?"

'Special agent Carter. He's been watching our family for a while now."

"So why don't we just kill him and get him out the way?" replied Symone.

"Because we don't know what he has on our family or where he is keeping it at. Trust me, he made you when you came in here. So, I been hearing a lot about your five-man team. You been a part of this family for three years now and you're running four night clubs and doing good. I ain't going to talk about your body count or your team's."

Symone looked at him as he was talking.

"Lorenzo, where is all this coming from?"

He looked at Symone after taking a sip of his drink.

"Symone, Jamila won't always be around and I need you to be ready just in case anything happens, do you understand me?" asked Lorenzo. "You might have to step up one day."

"I understand."

"The deposits are at the front desk waiting for you."

"Okay and I left what I got from Cam at the front desk for you too."

"Good."

"I'll call you sometime this week, Symone," said Lorenzo.

"Okay."

Symone got up and walked off. She got the deposits from the desk, and went back to the Hummer where Slim Boogie was waiting for her.

"What Lorenzo talking about?" asked Slim.

"There was a special agent in there we were talking about, and how he might need me to step up, but that's a conversation for another day. Let's go make these deposits before the bank closes on us."

***

Jamila was standing up, looking in her bird cage, when Lorenzo walked in.

"What's up, Jamila?"

Without turning around, she said, "So I got a phone call today from Cello telling me Felipe's brother is out of prison and he's asking questions about me, and he killed Carlos. I'm telling you this because I don't know what the future holds."

"Jamila, won't you just leave for a little while? I can run things—plus I have Symone, and she been running things good on her side of town," replied Lorenzo.

"I'll think about it."

"Okay, what is his brother's name? I'll do a check on him."

"Deoblow."

"Okay, I'll check him out."

"Good, did you give Symone the deposits?" asked Jamila

"Yea, we did that."

"Okay, I'm going to take care of some things. Can you close up for me, Lorenzo?"

"Yea, I can, Jamila."

"Okay."

"You are the Queen Don. You can't be riding around by yourself. You are a target if the wrong person sees you."

"I'll have Masi come with me."

"Thank you, Jamila!"

SAYNOMORE

Chapter 3

One Week Later—

"Can I take your order, sir?"

"Can you please tell me what are the specials for today?" asked the man.

"Sure, I can. We have steak with butter that's been sitting over a week with the secret sauce. And it is very slowly cooked with a sprinkle of powdered cheese on it for three hundred dollars. We have lobster with seven other fish stuffed in its tail with the house secret sauce for two hundred and fifty dollars."

"It sounds too good to be true. I'll take both of them."

"Oh, sir, we do ask that you pay up front," the waiter said.

"No problem. Can I pay in cash?"

'Sure, sir, and your meal will be out in twenty to thirty minutes, sir."

"Okay, thank you!"

Jamila walked in wearing a green dress hugging her body. She had on a diamond tennis bracelet on her left wrist with two-inch money green open-toe heels on. Her hair was pressed down with curls at the tip. She had a diamond choker necklace on too. Her dress had a slit going up the right and left thighs. Deoblow couldn't help but look at her, lusting over her as she walked past him.

"Excuse me, missus, may I please have a word with you?"

Jamila stopped and looked at him.

"Sure, anyone who eats here can have a word with me. May I take a seat?" asked Jamila.

"Please," replied Deoblow.

Deoblow got up and pulled her chair out for her.

"Thank you, so how may I help you?"

"First, I would like to say you have a beautiful place here."

"Thank you."

"Second, I would like to ask you something, do you know a Felipe Conway?" asked Deoblow.

Jamila looked at him with a smirk.

"Yes, I do know Felipe Conway, Mr. Deoblow. Is that why you came all the way from Mexico to ask me did I know your older brother? Or whether I killed your brother, Mr. Deoblow?"

He just looked at Jamila with a deadly glare.

"You ain't think I knew who you were?" said Jamila. "I made you and your men when you all walked through the door. I saw when all five of you walked in here and went to different tables. Even the two rented cars you have outside. I have eyes on them too. Take a look around, Mr. Deoblow, I have men at every corner looking at you and your men, ready to put all of you in black bags."

Jamila paused and smiled faintly. "Now let me see if I can remember this right, in this life we live, loved ones die all the time. Now listen to me, I'm not Carlos I don't plan on dying no time soon."

"I see why my brother was killed, he underestimated you," replied Deoblow.

"No, your brother was killed because he killed my father. In this life anybody gets killed if they move the pieces on the chess board in the right place."

Jamila put her finger in the air, and snapped them. A waiter walked up to her, handing her a white envelope with Deoblow's money inside, even the money his men spent on the meals they ordered.

"Here is the money you and your men spent on the meals, now you and your guys can leave," Jamila said to Deoblow.

Jamila snapped her fingers one more time, and her men walked up to each table Deoblow's men were at. Deoblow got up and fixed his tie. "Take care, Mrs. LaCross," he said as Jamila's men walked him to the door, out to his car. Jamila walked outside, and watched as they drove off.

"What you think, boss?"

"She's good, she's smart, maybe too smart. She knew I was coming the whole time. Let's put one million on her head."

"Done, I'll get right on it, sir."

Chapter 4

Everyone was sitting quietly at *Jelani's*. Jamila got up and looked around the table at everyone. No one said a word, as Jamila walked around the table and stopped at an empty seat.

"Can someone tell me where Cam is at?"

"With the rest of them who were disloyal to this family," said Symone before sitting back down.

"So, we have one seat to fill because of disloyalty. I want ya to hear what I'm about to say. You only get one chance with me before your life is taken, so think about the choices you make. I called this meeting because I'm about to leave for a few weeks. In my absence, Lorenzo will be the acting Don over the family, and Symone will be his number two. We are one family. This is not a black mafia family. Just because I'm black don't mean nothing. Look around at each other here. There is every race at this table and we run sixty-five percent of NYC. Let me make this clear, if I find out anybody went against Lorenzo or Symone, mark my word—you will have a horrible death, that I promise you. I don't want no one here to try and be brave while I'm gone. If there is a problem, report it to Lorenzo or Symone. Remember, it isn't important to come out on top, what matters is to come out alive. We are a family at this table—brothers and sisters. Everything I did, I did it for us. Everyone here will get a locket with a black diamond in it; you will never take it off. Lorenzo, if you don't mind—"

Lorenzo got up, picked up the bag next to his seat, and walked around the table, giving everyone a locket before taking his seat.

Jamila continued: "I need you to understand that the way you move will affect everyone at this table. Your actions will have a domino effect on everyone." She paused, looking around deliberately. "Does anybody see Elisha? No. And do you know why?" Everyone shook their heads by way of an answer to her question. "Well, it's because of his actions. With that being said, I have one more gift for everyone at this table. Symone, if you don't mind—"

Symone got up with the bag in her hand, and handed everyone an envelope with $20,000 in it.

"Now, you remember what I said," Jamila stressed.

Jamila looked around one more time before walking off. Lorenzo got up and spoke. "Everyone, nothing has changed. Go back to your post. This meeting is over."

Chapter 5

Three Days Later—

Symone walked into *Destiny's* and went to the bar. Masi walked up behind her.

"Symone, can I have a word with you?"

"Yea, come on, let's walk to the back over there to that table."

Sitting down, Symone looked around to see who all was in the bar before talking.

"What's up, Masi?"

"Word on the streets is that Jamila has one million dollars on her head right now."

"What! Who you heard that from?" asked Symone with a look of concern.

"One of the members from the Scott family was at the gambling spots drunk as fuck playing poker. I was standing behind him when he was talking about it."

"Masi, I want to hear word for word what he said."

"This is how he said it: *There was a meeting last night and Felipe's brother is out of prison. He found out Red Invee had his brother killed, so he put one million dollars on her head.* So, the dude he was with asked if there was a deadline. He said no. According to him, Felipe's brother added that if it's done by the end of next month, he's putting a hundred kilos on top of the one million dollars. That's when I walked away before I was seen."

"How many was there when he was talking to him? I mean how many guys around?"

"He was just talking to one guy, that's all," replied Masi.

Symone licked her lips. "Okay. Thank you!"

"I'll catch up with you later."

Symone pulled out her phone and called Lorenzo a few times, but he didn't pick up, so she got in her car and drove off. She went by *Jelani's*, and he wasn't there or at the waste plant. It's been two days, and she ain't hear from him. Symone was still thinking about what Masi said when her phone went off, and she saw it was Crystal calling her.

"Hello."

"Symone, I can't talk long, but listen to me, Lorenzo's fingerprints just came back."

"What you mean they just came back?" asked Symone.

"Two days ago, he was beaten real bad and taken to the hospital. They had him down as a John Doe. Once they ran his fingerprints, a red flag popped up and then it came to my department."

"Why did a red flag pop up?"

"Because they know he is a part of the LaCross family as Red Invee's second-in-command," replied Crystal.

"And what you mean he was beaten real bad?"

"Whoever got to him tried to kill him, Symone."
"Okay. What hospital is he at?"

"Southside Hospital."

"Okay, let me check on him. Thank you, Crystal!"

"No problem."

Symone pulled up at the hospital and walked to the front desk.

"Hello, I'm here to see Lorenzo LaCross."

"And you are?"

"His sister—Symone."

"Okay, he's in room 213 on the second floor."
"Thank you!"

Symone opened the door and walked in to see that Lorenzo was beaten badly. She looked at him lying supine in the bed, hooked up to IV's.

"Damn, what happened to you? Who did this to you, bro?" said Symone, as she touched his hand. He opened his eyes, looked at Symone, and said: "Detective Boatman," before passing out again.

"I'll take care of him, bro, I promise he's going to pay for this one," stated Symone.

That's when the doctor walked in. "Hello, who are you?"

"I'm his sister—Symone."

"Good, we've been trying to locate his family for the past two days now," said the doctor.

"Can you tell me what happened to him?"

"He came in this way. He was beaten badly. He has three broken ribs, a very bad concussion. His right arm is broken, and we have him on medication to help with the pain. He's been going in and out."

"Is he going to make it?" asked Symone.

"Yes, he is, but it's going to be a while before he's up and running again. We are talking about a few months. There have been a few officers here to talk to him, but every time they come in, he is asleep."

"Doctor, can I talk to you in private please?"

"Sure, follow me to my office. We can talk in there. It's right this way. Please come in and have a seat."

Symone watched as he took a seat behind his desk.

"So, tell me, how can I help you?"

Symone looked at him, "Doctor, my name is Symone LaCross. My sister's name is Jamila LaCross, do you know who we are?"

The doctor's eyes got big when she said that. He nodded, "Yes."

"Here's the deal, doctor. I will pay you sixty thousand dollars to take care of him, but not here. I need you to help me move him somewhere else."

"Where do you want him moved to?"

Symone wrote an address down and handed it to the doctor.

"I need him moved to that address. Can you have that done?"

"Sure, I can."

"When can you do it?"

"I can try and have it done tomorrow night."

Okay, I'll be there waiting on you—and please, doctor, don't let me down."

"I'll try not to."

"Good, I'll have your money when you get there tomorrow, and I don't want nobody to know where he was moved to."

"I understand."

Symone got up and walked out of the office to the waiting room. She stopped by the candy machine. That's when she saw Detective Boatman in the reflection of the glass standing behind her. She turned around to face him.

"It's a shame what happened to Lorenzo."

"It is, but every dog has his day," replied Symone.

"Symone, I haven't seen your sister Jamila in a while, where is she?" asked Detective Boatman with a smirk on his face.

"I don't know," replied Symone, looking at him eye to eye, not lowering her gaze. "Didn't you get the last message my sister left you? I think she left it with your brother."

"I did get that message. Now, make sure she gets the message I left with Lorenzo. And tell her Mr. Deoblow sends his best regards. I'll be in touch, Symone."

Symone watched as he walked off. Symone pulled out her phone and called Slim Boogie.

"Hey, what's up, Symone?"

"Call everyone and have them at *Passions* tonight by eight p.m. Tell them to wear gray."

"I'm on it now."

Symone hung up the phone. All that was going through her mind was that there was one million dollars on Jamila's head and she'd been gone for three months. Lorenzo was half dead. There was a detective trying to put the press down on her. And on top of all that, now she had all the businesses to run. It was time to really turn into a boss bitch and find out who took the contract out on her sister. And it was necessary to find out why the Scott family was the first to know about it, and what ties they have with Deoblow.

Chapter 6

"Mr. Scott, you have a Mr. Deoblow here to see you, sir."

"Send him back."

"Yes, sir."

"Mr. Deoblow, he said come on back."

Mr. Scott got up and walked over to shake Mr. Deoblow's hand. "Mr. Deoblow, it's nice to meet you."

"Likewise, Mr. Scott."

"Please have a seat. So, I'm very interested in the contract on Red Invee," stated Mr. Scott.

"Mr. Scott, I don't know this name Red Invee."

"Because you know her better as Jamila LaCross. So, tell me the details to this contract. One million dollars plus one hundred kilos of pure cocaine, hundred percent pure."

"So, tell me, Mr. Scott, what can you tell me about Red Invee?" asked Deoblow.

"She is very smart and has a lot of strong ties with a lot of important people. But I don't like the nigga, and I don't like the fact they let a nigga become the head Don. So, I been wanting the bitch dead for a very long time. She has been a pest in my backyard for a very long time. A few other families feel the same way."

"So, what makes you think you can kill this pest as you said it?"

"Because I believe anybody can get killed, and I do mean *anybody*."

Mr. Scott watched as Deoblow lit his cigar.

"So, tell me, Mr. Scott, what makes you think you can do what Tony or Deniro couldn't?"

"Because they let her know they were coming. I'll get her and them nigga lovers in the blind."

"So are you saying I can put my trust in you?"

"I'll say let's drink to that and a new friendship."

Mr. Scott got up and poured two shots of Brandy for both of them.

***

Symone walked into *Passions* wearing a gray chinchilla and a gray skirt with three-inch black heels. She had on a gray shirt, and her hair was pulled back. Masi pulled her chair out for her when she walked to the table. She took her seat and looked around.

"There are new rules starting now tonight. Someone is trying to break our family up one by one. So we are going to show these mothafuckers we are not to be fucked with. I don't care if we have to kill everyone that I think is against us one by one. We are about to set NYC on fire, and this gray represents us because we are gonna be the last ones standing when the flames go out. Masi, show them the pictures."

Masi showed everyone the pictures. Then Symone explained:

"These pictures are of Donnie Scott and Joe Scott. Donnie was the one running his mouth off about the hit on Jamila. So we need to know what he knows. Joe runs that gambling spot downtown and since they think shit is sweet, I want part of it now. We are going to paint NYC red to let everyone know we are not to be fucked with."

"Symone, you know this could start a war."

"KT, the war started when the contract went on Jamila's life. So, we are going to cut the head off the snake and watch the body fall. It's no secret that Joe wants to be the head of the Scott family, so we are going to push the issue. We are trying to make them feel the heat we are spitting out. It's time. So, Masi and Slim Boogie, I need Detective Boatman dead. You two get in town with Crystal and tell her I need to see her asap. From here on out I'm a ghost. To talk to me, you will go through Masi or Slim Boogie. I want everyone at the nightclubs—*Jelani's* and *Destiny's*. Remember when they made our guns, they made theirs, and I don't want nobody in black bags from this family. Kill or be killed, is all you need to remember. Masi and Slim, I don't care how you do it, but get me Donnie and I need it done without being loud with it. When you get him, bring him to the plant and ya remember this, if anyone of ya run your fucking mouth off, I'll kill your whole fucking family one by one—I promise you that! Meeting's over."

Chapter 7

"Donnie, you need to stop drinking so much."

"Why do my drinking bother you?"

"No, but you never know what could happen."

"I ain't worried about nothing, Joe," said Donnie.

"You should be. You was talking real loud the other night at the spot."

"You mean about that nigga—Jamila? Fuck her, fuck her. Bartender, get me another drink."

"No, he had enough."

"I'm a grown ass man. Who are you to tell me when I had enough?"

"You know what?" replied Joe. "Drink your ass in a fucking coma, I'm leaving."

"So why are you still here? Bartender, that drink."

Joe hit the bar with his fist and walked off. Two hours passed and Donnie was still there drinking.

"Hey, let me get another drink."

"Donnie, it's eleven forty-five p.m. We close in fifteen minutes. The bar is closed."

"Okay, what's my tab?" asked Donnie.

"Sixty dollars."

"Here's a hundred dollars, keep the change."

Donnie got up and walked out the bar, holding on to the wall, drunk. As he pulled out his lighter so he can light his cigarette, he dropped his lighter on the ground. He reached down to pick it up as he stumbled to his car. That's when Slim Boogie hit him over the head with a billy club, knocking him out cold.

"Come on, Masi, let's get him in the trunk of the car."

"What this fat muthafucker weigh?"

"I don't know, too fucking much, Slim."

They dropped him in the trunk of the car and drove off. Once at the plant, they tied him up to a chair and put a paper bag over his head.

***

It was 2 p.m. the next afternoon; Symone walked into the plant.

"How long he's been here for?"

"We got him last night around twelve midnight."

"Okay, Slim. Masi, go get me a bucket of cold water."

Symone walked over to him, and took the bag off his head. She was looking at his red face as he was still knocked out cold.

"Here you go, Symone."

"Thank you, Masi!"

She took the bucket of water and threw it on him, waking him up.

"What the fuck, what the fuck, where am I?" asked Donnie.

"You are with me, Donnie, so let's make this quick. All I want to know is what you know, that's all."

"Fuck you, nigga, I ain't telling you shit."

Symone ain't say a word. She just walked up to Donnie with her gun in her hand and shot him in the knee cap. Donnie let out a scream.

"You fucking nigga! You are dead, I swear."

Symone shot him in the other knee.

"Fuck, fuck, okay, okay, what you want to know?" screamed Donnie in pain.

"Who put the money on my sister's head?"

"Deoblow, one million dollars."

"Who else know about this hit?" asked Symone.

"Just my family," said Donnie as tears came from his eyes.

Symone looked at the tears and sweat coming down his face.

"Donnie, I need to know—how can I get in touch with Joe?"

"Fuck you, nigga, I ain't telling you shit else."

Masi looked at Symone, and then went to walk up to Donnie, but Symone stopped him.

"I got this, hand me those pliers."

Slim Boogie handed her the pliers, as she walked up to Donnie.

"So you don't want to talk, don't worry about it then."

"Fuck you, nigga!" spat Donnie.

Symone smacked him in the face with the pliers, then got on top of him, and started pulling his teeth out.

"Who the fuck you think you talking to, cracker? I'm the right bitch! Fuck dying fast, you going to die in fucking pain. Now tell me where the fuck Joe is at!" she yelled at him as he was kicking his legs, blood coming out his mouth. She then grabbed the top part of his ear and ripped it off with the pliers.

"Get me them bolt cutters. I want his fingers now."

"Wait, wait, wait!" Donnie cried out with blood coming from his mouth. "He's always at the gambling club. He never really leaves there. Please don't hurt me no more. I'm telling you the truth."

"I still don't believe you." Symone walked behind him and cut his fingers off, two of them.

"Ahhh, I'll fucking kill you!"

Symone looked at him as he started to pass out from the pain and loss of blood.

"Donnie, don't pass out on me yet, we just getting started. Slim Boogie, Masi—the crowbar and baseball bat is right there. Beat him to death now."

Symone sat down and watched as Slim Boogie beat Donnie with the crowbar over and over again. And when he wasn't beating him, Masi was. Symone watched till she couldn't see his face no more. They took Donnie, put him in the trunk of his car, drove it under the bridge and set it on fire.

"Symone, you ready?"

"No, I want to see the car in full flames, then I will be ready."

She was smoking a *black-n-mild* until she walked over to the car and flicked it into the flames.

"Now I'm ready."

Masi and Slim Boogie just watched Symone the whole time until she got in the car.

SAYNOMORE

Chapter 8

Paul was talking on the phone when Joe walked in. He put his finger up to tell him to hold on one second. Joe walked over to the bar and got two glasses and a bottle of Brandy, and took a seat in front of Paul's desk. Paul hung the phone up. "What the drinks for?"

"It's for Donnie. The police just found his car, and his body was in the trunk of it—burnt to a crisp when they found his car."

"I just got the phone call. Not only that, he also had fingers cut off and his right ear was missing."

Paul let out a heavy sigh before he continued: "So, besides the torture they subjected him to, they torched him."

"Yea, they did, Paul."

"Who you think did this?"

"I don't know but someone just sent us a message."

"Joe, find out who did this and whoever did this—I want them dead."

Paul reached in his drawer, pulled out his lighter and lit his cigar.

"Joe, get me Boatman down here now."

***

"How is he doing, doctor?"

"He's coming along good."

Symone rubbed her hand along Lorenzo's head. "Don't worry, Lorenzo, I'm here now. I got you." Symone looked at the doctor. "Here you go, doctor, sixty thousand dollars in cash."

"Thank you!"

"I have to go, but if you need anything, call this number."

Symone walked out the door, picked up the phone, and called Slim.

"Did you send that off yet?"

"Yea, I did that yesterday morning," replied Slim.

"Okay, I was just making sure. You and Masi, meet me at *Passions* at eight p.m. tonight."

"Okay, I'll call Masi now."

Slim walked to his Hummer and called Masi.

"Yo, what's up, Boogie?"

"Shit, look, Symone wants us to come to *Passions* tonight around eight p.m."

"Say no more, I'll be there, peace," replied Masi.

"A'ight, bro."

***

Paul was sitting on his desk, eating an apple, when Boatman walked in.

"It's about time you got here."

"What's going on?" asked Boatman.

"Someone killed one of my guys, and I need to know who."

"I heard you. When a name comes up, I got you, but right now it's like going on a witch hunt, Paul."

"Mr. Scott, sir, this package just came in."

"Who sent it?"

"It don't say."

"Okay, place it over there. Now what was you saying about witch hunts, Boatman?"

"I lost my train of thoughts—Paul, someone just sent you that with no return address—I think you might want to open it up," replied Boatman.

Paul got up and picked up the box. He placed his ear to the box to see if he could hear a clicking sound before he opened it up. He looked at Detective Boatman when he opened up the box. It had Donnie's three fingers and ear in it with a note that said, "I hear everything."

"What the fuck! Paul, someone was talking and their voice got out."

"Boatman, find out who the fuck did this now."

"I will. Let me take that box off your hands."

Boatman took the box and walked out of Paul's office.

Chapter 9

Symone was sitting down looking at a picture of her and Jamila, when Slim Boogie and Masi walked in.

"What's up, Symone?"

"I been doing a lot of thinking about what Masi asked me. I found out that Joe owns that night spot and he makes close to one million dollars every three days from the gambling they do in there. But it's not just his, the Scott family owns thirty percent, but Joe got the other seventy percent. So, ya get ready, we are going to pay him a visit, I want it all."

"So we are going to go to his club?"

"No, we are going to go to his penthouse downtown and pay him a late-night visit."

That's when there was a knock at the door. Symone looked to see Muscle opening the door.

"Excuse me, Symone, Crystal is here to see you."

"Okay, let her in. Slim and Masi, I will call you two later."

Crystal walked in looking shocked and confused.

"Hello, Crystal, please come in and have a seat. Can I get you some wine or water?" asked Symone.

"No, thank you."

"So how you been, Crystal?"

"Good and yourself?"

"I been good, but I asked you to come because I need a problem taken care of.

"And what's that?" asked Crystal.

"Detective Boatman, do you know him?"

"Yea, I do, he's a pain in my ass."

"Well, Crystal, he needs to disappear for good."

"Are you asking me to kill a cop?"

"Yea, I am," replied Symone. "I know you can get close to him."

"Symone, I never killed no one before."

"Well, it's time to break the ice, beautiful."

"When you want this done?"

"Saturday."

Symone looked in Crystal's face and saw she couldn't do it.

"Look, Crystal, just have him meet you in the Bronx and I'll have someone else do the dirty work. Did you receive your package this month?"

"Yes, I have."

"Okay, just making sure. Crystal, call me when you are ready."

"Where do you want me to have him meet me at in the Bronx?"

Symone quickly fetched a pen and a piece of paper. She scribbled something on the paper and handed it to Crystal. "Have him meet you *here*—"

Crystal looked at the paper and nodded as she got up. She walked out, pronto. Symone lit her *black-n-mild,* and watched as Crystal walked out the door.

***

"Joe, you think someone tipped Jamila off about the hit?"

"I don't know, Paul, no one seen Jamila in over three weeks."

"I know Detective Boatman beat Lorenzo into a coma two and a half weeks ago with the intent to find out where she is."

"So, who is running the family now, Paul?"

"I heard it was Symone. You know what? Let's give her a little gift."

"What you had in mind, Paul?"

"Put a bomb in her car and shoot that nigga's club up—*Passions*—she runs. And if I find out it was her who killed Donnie, I'll skin that nigga alive. Get on that, now."

***

"Symone, it looks like a big crowd tonight."

"Yea, we are close to five hundred people, Slim."

"So how you holding up with all this pressure on you, Symone?"

"I'm just trying to walk in my sister's footsteps, and I always ask myself *what would she do?*"

"Symone, we need to have a heart to heart."

Symone looked at Slim. "What's up? What's on your mind, Slim?"

"Four years ago, before we was a part of the LaCross family, you wasn't like this. You bodied twenty-plus people already, everyone knows who you are. Your sister kills when she has too, not like you."

"I do what I have to do to make my point, so what's your point, Slim?" asked Symone.

Look, it took your sister years to build this empire up. Don't knock it down in a few months. Paul going to figure it out it was us, and he's going to hit back, trust me on that."

"I don't care if he do. This will be all over in a few weeks," said Symone.

"You can't say that," replied Slim.

"Why can't I?"

"Because when you get ready to stop, they might just be ready to begin, just think about that. Look, it's three-thirty a.m. I'm about to go downstairs and close up the place. I'll be back up here in a few."

"Hey, Slim Boogie."

"Yea."

"You always going to have my back, right?"

"Yea, they kill you, they kill me," said Slim as he walked out the door. It was 4 a.m. when they closed up the place.

"Slim, walk me to my car."

"Come on."

"So what you about to do, Slim?"

"I don't know yet, but my bed sounds like a plan."

Symone walked to the edge of the curb, and pressed her alarm on her car as she was looking at Slim Boogie. That's when her car blew up, hurling her and Slim against the wall of the club. That's when two gunshots erupted, and two cars drove by—shooting assault rifles, hitting everything. Symone was lying down unconscious, and Slim dragged her inside. People were on the floor, crying. Some were yelling and screaming. All one saw was blue and red lights flashing. Slim got Symone to her office and laid her down. Then he ran back downstairs out the door, where the police were at. His head was pounding and ears ringing. He looked at the cars that were on fire, even the three people that were hit lying on the ground. It was six that morning before the police was gone and the fire was out.

Chapter 10

Symone woke up the following afternoon. She was in Slim Boogie's bed. She had a very bad headache. Looking around the room her, eyesight was blurry. She got up and walked downstairs where Slim was seated watching the news.

"I see you are up."

"What happened last night?" asked Symone.

"You was almost killed. They put a bomb in your car."

Symone pulled out a chair from the table.

"Let me make some coffee," said Slim.

"Thank you."

"Here you go, and here is something for your head."

"So they put a bomb in my car?"

"Yes, they did, but they must have rigged it up wrong because it went off when you hit your alarm. They also shot up *Passions* and three people got hit last night. The windows were shot out. It was a mess."

"Oh my God, so the windows are broken?" asked Symone.

"Yes, but don't worry. I took care of that already. I have Masi and Muscle down there getting the repairs done. So, I'm guessing Paul figured it out like I said he would, Symone."

"Slim, what time is it?"

"It's going on three p.m."

"I need you to take me to my house. I need to take a shower and go check on Lorenzo."

"Symone, you need to relax, you almost was killed last night. You should be lucky you don't have no broken bones. If you was a little closer to that car, you would have been dead."

"I know, Slim, but I can't let that stop me."

"Symone, shit got real last night."

"I know, Slim, so from here on out we need to make them feel our pain. Henceforth, we play for keeps, we will make them hurt like never before.

***

Paul sat on his desk with one leg hanging off of it, resting his hands on his leg, looking at everyone standing around in his office. "I called all of you here because as of right now, I know you all heard of how Donnie was killed. And no one in this family will get killed without someone dying with them. So, I know Red Invee's little sister—Symone—had something to do with what happened to Donnie. So, I had her club hit last night. As of right now, we are at war with the LaCross family." Paul got up from his desk and eyed everyone.

"And we will not end up like Felipe, Tony or Deniro in a pine fucking box. If you see any of the LaCross family members, you shoot them on sight. I don't give a fuck who they are with. Joe, you keep an eye out on Jamila. Detective Boatman, you take care of Symone."

"Paul, Boatman beat Lorenzo to a coma, almost half to death, and he still wouldn't say where Jamila was at. It's been over a month and nobody has seen her at all."

"Joe, I don't care who you have to talk with. Just find the bitch and get it done. Now, everyone, leave me. I have nothing else to say.

***

"Hey Lorenzo, are you going to open your eyes for me today?" said Symone, as she rubbed her hand over his head lightly.

Symone turned around as she heard the door open, and the doctor walked in.

"Hello, Symone."

"Hey, how is he doing?"

"He is getting there, but like I said—it's a slow process, but all his vital signs are good."

"Is there anything that you need?" asked Symone.

"I need some help with him, maybe a nurse who can sit with him more throughout the day," replied the doctor.

"Okay, here you go—this is ten thousand dollars for a nurse that can help you, but make sure you can trust her because her life depends on it."

"You have my word. I understand very clearly."

"Okay, I have some runs to make, so I'll see you later," said Symone.

"I'll have someone here when you get back."

Symone walked out to the living room where Slim Boogie was waiting on her at.

"So what now, Symone?"

"Call Masi. I want everyone at *Destiny's* within two hours with their guns fully loaded. We are going to pay Paul a visit tonight."

"Where at?" asked Slim.

"Where else? That fucking club he owns up town."

"I'm about to call him now."

"Good."

***

It was 10:35 p.m. when Symone had six cars pulled up in front of Paul's club. Symone stepped out the car, looking like a cover girl model, wearing all black and gray. She looked at the men Paul had watching the front door, but Symone had four men in the waiting line to get in the club already. When Paul's men reached for their guns, Symone's men had their guns to their heads already. Symone walked up to them.

"Slim, Masi and Muscle, take their weapons from them and if they move the wrong way, kill them."

Symone walked past them as two of her men opened the door for her to walk in. Symone had fifteen of her guys walking in alongside their with her guns out. The music stopped playing, as everyone watched Symone walk in the club right up to the VIP, where Paul was sitting. His men made a move to reach for their guns, but he had told them not to. He knew at that time they had no chance in that gun fight. Everyone moved out the way when Symone walked up and took a seat next to Paul. Paul picked up his glass of Brandy and took a sip. Muscle looked at Paul's second-in-command and the bodyguards standing next to Paul.

"How may I help you, Symone?"

"Your shots fucking missed."

"I don't know what you are talking about," replied Paul.

Symone looked at him, and crossed her legs. "I think you do know what I'm talking about, Paul, but trust me—if I wanted to kill you, it would be easy with men like this at your front door."

Paul looked at his men that were at the front door with guns to their heads. Slim Boogie pushed two of them on the floor in front of Paul, and Masi did the same thing to the men he himself had held under the control of his gun, looking at Paul—ready for anything. Paul put his glass down, and looked at Symone. "You are right. They could have cost me my life." He pulled his gun out and shot them all in the head at point-blank range.

Symone looked at him, then picked up his drink and took the last shot. Masi watched him as he put his gun back up.

"Paul, just know my shooters don't miss. Next time it will be your body lying on the floor in a pool of blood, let this be the first and last warning."

After issuing that warning, Symone got up and walked out.

"Hey, Symone," yelled Paul, "where is that sister of yours? She been missing for a month now. Nobody seen her." He gave a short laugh.

She turned around and smiled with a smirk on her face. Then she looked at Masi and Slim Boogie, and nodded at them. Paul looked at them as they raised their guns.

"Get down, get down!" yelled Paul, as they shot the club up, hitting the DJ booth, tables, windows. Paul and his men were on the floor, holding their heads until the shooting stopped. When he got up off the floor, Symone and her men were gone. There were holes in the walls, broken windows and seven people were dead all over the floor. Paul was screaming and yelling.

***

"Symone, what is next?"

"Whatever comes our way, Masi, we are going to paint NYC red. The Scott family wants smoke, so we are going to burn them the fuck up. The flames are going to be real hot!"

"You should have just killed him right there when you had the chance, we had him down bad," replied Masi.

"I know, but it is what it is. He got an understanding now that I'm not playing with him."

SAYNOMORE

Chapter 11

"Paul, what happened out there last night?"

"That nigga came to my fucking club and killed seven of my men. She shot that bitch the fuck up and walked out of the club."

"Paul, we need to get them in the blind—We need to have a sit-down with her to win this war," replied Joe.

"I'll have a sit-down when I'm looking over her dead, lifeless body. I remember back in the days—you can pay someone six hundred to a thousand dollars, and one or maybe two days, the problem was gone."

"Paul, we can't kill her yet, she's the only one who knows where Red Invee is at."

"Joe, I remember times when people feared the Scott family. Just that name alone—just our presence—moved crowds. Our family was the family that made people have nightmares, fuck! Okay, Joe, set up a meeting and let's see where this goes. I can't believe I'm about to have a sit down with a nigga! Is this what the Mafia became? Damn!"

"I'll get on it first thing in the morning, Paul." Joe walked out Paul's office, leaving him in his thoughts.

***

"Symone, what's wrong? What's on your mind?" asked Masi.

Symone was looking out the window at the rain. She reached in her bag and pulled out a *black-n-mild*, lowering her head as she lit it.

"Masi," said Symone as she blew the smoke out her mouth, "I want them to respect me and what I stand on even if I have to turn March into a month of murders. But first, we need to get Boatman out the way and I want to know what he has on our family."

"Facts, how is Lorenzo doing?"

"He's coming along. It was worse than what the doctor thought, but he's going to be alright. Right now, I need you and Slim Boogie to be on your jobs. I want Boatman dead."

"We on that. I promise you that, Symone."

"Good."

Symone opened up Masi's car door and got out. She dropped her *black-n-mild* in a puddle of water, and walked to her door. Masi watched her till she went inside before he drove away.

Chapter 12

"Yo, Muscle, come look at this."

Muscle replied: "Look at what, KT? What the fuck! You know they in the wrong spot. Come on, KT, guns up."

As they walked downstairs to the bar, KT looked at the two strangers. "Ya lost?"

"No, we need to talk. Is there some place we can talk?"

Muscle looked at KT, then said to the two strangers: "Yea, follow me to the office."

KT just watched as they walked behind Muscle to the office.

"Now tell me, what can I do for you?"

"Paul wants to have a sit-down with the LaCross family this week."

"We have to ask Symone, but if she agrees—when and where?"

"Tuesday at three p.m., and we can have it here."

"No, we will meet at *Jelani's*. Is there a number we can contact you on if she decides to have this meeting?"

"Sure, here is Mr. Scott's card."

I'll give it to her. You two have a good day. KT, you can show them out."

***

Symone looked in the mirror after her shower. As water dripped down her face, she thought about what she was turning into. That's when her phone went off. She walked to the bed to see it was Muscle calling her.

"What's up, Muscle?" asked Symone.

"I was calling you to let you know we had two visitors come by the club today."

"Who was they?"

"Two members of the Scott family came by. They want to have a meeting Tuesday at *Jelani's*."

"About what?" replied Symone.

"We ain't get into all of that."

"What time do they want to have this meeting?"

"Three p.m. They also offered me his card to give you in case you say yea, so you can call and let them know it's a go."

"No, Muscle, you call and let them know, and make sure we have extra men outside and inside. I want eyes everywhere."

"Okay, I'll make sure everyone is set up right."

"Good, I'll go check up on Lorenzo and I'll see you tomorrow at two p.m. at *Jelani's*"

"Okay, I'll see you then, Symone."

***

"Carlito, how long it's been since our talk with the Scott family?"

"About four weeks now, Mr. Deoblow. How long before they get the job done?"

"I don't know, she is very smart, Carlito. If it was like throwing a rock in a lake, she would have been dead by now. I don't understand how they let a female get so powerful in a few years."

"Mr. Deoblow, she is good at what she does. The same way she sat at this table with your brother, walked around the track with him, and this is how they had him killed. Did you give the Scott family a deadline?"

Deoblow shook his head. "No, but I hope they get it done in the next few weeks. If not, I'm pulling the contract off her head and I'm putting it on Paul's head. If he ain't deliver on his word, then he is a dead man."

Deoblow took his sip of Brandy, then pulled out his cigar and a lighter.

***

Symone put on some pink and white three-inch Timberland boots with matching sweatpants and hoodie, and an all-white bomber jacket. She drove around Queen's for over an hour before she pulled in where Lorenzo was at. She made sure she checked on him every day. It's been over two months since he was jumped on and left for dead. When she walked in the house, he was sitting up in the bed, looking at the news.

"Thank God, Lorenzo, you are okay. I was worried sick about you."

Symone walked up to him and gave him a hug and kiss on the cheek.

"Symone, thank you for everything!"

"No problem, you are my brother."

"I see our little talk we had a few days before I got jumped paid off."

"Yea, a lot has happened since you been hospitalized. How long you been up for?" asked Symone.

"Three—maybe four—hours," said Lorenzo.

"How do you feel?"

"Like I been ran over by a heavy-duty truck three times back-to-back."

"Where is the doctor at?" replied Symone.

"He stepped out to go get something for me. I'm on so much pain meds right now I can't feel anything. So what's been going on? What I miss?"

"A lot has happened since you been here," said Symone. "But first, tell me what happened to you?"

"I went to the Bronx to go see an old friend of mine like always. I cut through the alley. That's when I heard a voice and when I turned around, it was Detective Boatman. He must have been following me. He asked me where Jamila was at. I told him I don't know. That's when I was just walking away and was hit in the back of the head with a pipe. I hit the ground and before I knew it, it was three more guys jumping on me with bats and chains, asking me where is Jamila at. I remember one guy picked me up and asked me where she at again. I looked at Boatman and when he was close enough, I spit in his face and said: *Fuck you.* That's when I felt two sharp blows to my ribs, and I went down again. I saw one of the guys pull out a gun and pointed it right at my head. I looked to the side and saw blue and red lights. That's when I passed out. I'm thinking someone called the police because they stopped right in front of the alley."

"I'm glad you are okay. So since you been gone, there have been a lot of deaths, and we are at war with the Scott family right now. I found out there is a contract on Jamila right now for one million dollars and the Scott family took the contract out on her. I killed Donnie, and they shot up *Passions*. So, I went and shot up Paul's night club. So now they want to have a meeting. I have a meeting with Paul at three p.m. at *Jelani's*."

"Do you need me there?" asked Lorenzo.

"No, I don't want nobody to know you are okay until you are at hundred percent again."

"Symone, you remind me of Jamila right now."

"Don't worry about Boatman. He will be taken care of this weekend. And—Lorenzo—I don't want you telling Jamila nothing. I will explain everything to her when she gets back."

"Symone, you have my word, I will keep quiet."

"Thanks, Lorenzo, I have to go. It's one-thirty and the meeting is at three p.m. I need to make sure everyone is ready just in case anything happens."

"Okay, I'll be here when you get back."

"Okay. I love you, Lorenzo!"

"I love you too, Symone."

Symone turned to leave the room, but stopped in her tracks when Lorenzo called her name.

"Symone?"

"Yes, Lorenzo." She looked back over her shoulder.

"I'm proud of you," exclaimed Lorenzo.

"Thanks," Symone smiled as she walked out.

***

Symone pulled up at *Jelani's*. Muscle and Masi were out front, watching the door. Slim Boogie came out the restaurant, walked to Symone's car, and opened the door for her as the valet got in her car to go park it.

"How you feeling, Symone?"

"Good, is everyone where they need to be?"

"Yes, I have men on the floor, two at every corner, and I have two more guys that's going to come out here to take Masi and Muscle's position so they can join us in the meeting."

"Good, how long before they get here?" asked Symone.

"Ten minutes at the most."

"Masi, Muscle, come on," replied Symone. "I'm telling y'all if these mothafuckers even blink the wrong way, cook their ass."

When Symone made it to the elevator, KT was standing there.

"KT, when they arrive, you bring them up to the office."

"Okay, I will."

Symone stepped on the elevator with Masi, Slim and Muscle. They headed to Jamila's office.

***

Paul pulled up and got out his limo together with four of his men. He fixed his tie as he stepped out.

"Come on, let's get this over with."

KT walked up to Paul and shook his hand.

"Hey, Symone is upstairs waiting for you now, follow me."

Paul had never been into *Jelani's*. He looked around at all the people eating and stopped when he saw a picture of Jamila and Jatavious Stone on the wall together at the Mayor's ball. He pointed the picture out to Joe. Three minutes later, they were walking through Jamila's office doors.

"Hello, gentlemen. Please have a seat, Paul."

"Thank you, but I'ma get to the point. I'll keep my men off your turf and you keep your men off my turf. I'm not going to act like I like you because I don't. But if it takes me to sit here and look in your face to keep a war from getting out of control, then so be it."

Symone pulled out her pack of *black-n-milds*, took one out and lit it. Muscle, Masi and Slim were looking at Paul's men, never taking their eyes off them.

"Paul, that goes both ways. I don't give two fucks about you at all. Now you saying stay on our side of town, but I know your family took out a contract on my sister, also known as the Queen Don. I need to know, is there any truth to this rumor? What you are asking, I cannot do. And there will be more blood on the streets of NYC."

Symone dumped the ashes in the ashtray from her *black-n-mild*.

"There is no truth to what you are asking me."

"I'm glad you said that. So, Mr. Paul, I will keep my guys from your side of town and you will keep your men from my side of town."

Paul stood up and adjusted his tie. Symone stood up, walked around Jamila's desk, and shook Paul's hand. "Have a nice afternoon, Paul."

"Likewise, Symone."

Paul and his men walked out the door as KT walked them out the restaurant.

"What you think, Symone?"

"He's lying about everything. He just wants us to put our guard down so he can strike, Slim."

"Symone, no disrespect, why you keep letting him walk away when we have him down bad?"

"Masi, stop questioning how I run this family and let that be the first and last time I tell you that. Now, if I would have killed him here, how would that had looked on our family? *The LaCross family had Paul Scott come to Jelani's and then had him killed*—that will be the talk of the town because everyone knows we was going to have a meeting with him today. It's about thinking, Masi, not killing all the time."

Chapter 13

It was 6:30 when Crystal called Symone.

"Hey, Symone, it's Crystal."

"What's up?" replied Symone.

"I just got a call from Boatman. He wants to meet me tonight."

"What! Crystal, why?"

"He said he got plans this weekend and won't be able to see me at all this weekend. Tonight is the only free night he has to see me."

"Okay. Look, Crystal, have him meet up with you in Bronx in front of Pandora's Box, and call me when his car pulls up. Do not get into his car at all."

"Okay, Symone, I'll tell him now."

Symone ran out the front door and went to a hole-in-the wall hardware shop, and got a bottle of lighter fluid, then parked three car-lengths down from Pandora's Box. Symone looked at her watch; it was 8:30 p.m. when she saw Boatman's car pull up. Twenty seconds later, Crystal called to let her know he was out front.

"I see him. Just stay inside." Symone watched as he rolled down the window and lit a cigarette. Crystal was watching everything from the window inside the building. Symone heard the music Boatman was playing. She looked around to see if anyone was around. She ain't see nobody in sight. It was quiet outside, besides the music that Boatman was playing. Symone walked up to the side of Detective Boatman's car. He was so busy messing with the car radio he ain't see it coming. When he turned around and looked up, Symone said: "Lorenzo sends his best wishes." Before he could blink, Symone was shooting him at point-blank range—three shots to the head and two shots to the chest. His lifeless body leaned over the passenger side of the car. Symone pulled out the lighter fluid and poured it all over his body. She lit the match and threw it on his body, then ran off. There was an old lady who came outside when she heard the gunshots; she saw the whole thing. Symone saw her as she ran past her. She made it back to her car. While she was pulling off, she stopped in front of the old lady and shot her two times in the face, killing her instantly. She drove off before the woman's body hit the ground. Symone drove to an abandoned parking lot, pulled her tags off, got her information, and set the car on fire. It was 1:30 a.m. when Symone made it back home. She knew what she did could get her a life sentence in prison, but she had to get it done.

Chapter 14

Joe walked into Paul's office as he was watching the news.

"I see you caught the news. You think it's the LaCross family?"

"What the fuck you think? A detective gets killed who works for me in front of one of my businesses, then they set him on fire. Yes, I think it was that little bitch. It was a message to say anyone can get killed. Then they killed the old lady, they put two in her head because she saw the whole fucking thing. No witness, no gun, they set the car on fire, no fingerprints, the perfect fucking crime. I'm really starting to grow a real fucking hate for the LaCross family and them nigga lovers!"

"So you do think it was them?" replied Joe.

"I wouldn't put it past them."

"You think Jamila had this done, Paul?"

She might have. She's been missing for over a month, then a detective gets killed. I wouldn't put it past her. This is going to be big, Joe, I guarantee that."

***

"Slim, Muscle, I need you two at *Destiny*'s tonight. Masi, you with me. KT, I want you on guard, meaning *watch out for Lorenzo*. I don't trust the Scott family at all."

"Okay. Symone, did you see the news? Detective Boatman got rolled last night the worst way."

"I know. I pushed his shit back, fuck him. Word got to me he was the one who jumped on Lorenzo, Masi. Just like I can't wait to roll Paul because I know he's waiting to see my lifeless body in a fucking casket. And we still need to move on Joe. I want that night spot and casino he has. My word is law until the Queen Don comes back."

Just at that moment, Jamila opened the door. Everyone turned around and looked at her in the doorway. She looked dead at Symone.

"I want a meeting at the plant tonight at seven-thirty, and I want everyone there and nobody better be late." Jamila looked at everyone one last time and walked out. "And remember I want to hear what you hear and see what you see."

It was 7:15 p.m. when Jamila walked in the room where everyone was sitting down already. She walked up to Lorenzo and gave him a kiss on the forehead, then walked up to Symone and patted her on the back. Finally, she walked to the head of the table and took her seat.

"I been gone a little over a month and within that time New York City became a war zone. It's been cop killings, clubs being shot up, over fifteen dead bodies and innocent people being killed. Slim, Masi, Muscle and KT, you have anything to say?"

Symone stood up. "No, *I* have something to say."

"Okay, can you please share it with me?"

"I found out there was a million dollars and hundred kilos on your head," stated Symone.

Jamila put her hand on her chest. "I'm flattered. Please continue, Symone."

"So I tried to call Lorenzo, but his phone was going right to voicemail. I went to all the businesses and couldn't find him. That's when Crystal called me and told me he was at the hospital."

Jamila looked over at Crystal. She placed her hands on the table as she got up, looking at everyone.

"I'm proud of all of you here for listening to Symone in my absence. As of right now, we are at war. Symone, did Paul set up a meeting with you yet?" asked Jamila.

"Yes, he did two days ago."

"What he say?"

"That he wants to end this war and that our guys will stay off his side of town and his guys will stay off our side of town," replied Symone.

"That's some bullshit. He's just trying to rock you to sleep. Okay, this is what I want everyone to do, go back to your post. I want two men at every door. This meeting is over and if it don't look right, then doormat their ass. Symone, Lorenzo, I'll like to speak to the both of you in private."

***

Jamila walked in her office, then closed the door once Lorenzo and Symone walked in.

"Symone," yelled Jamila, "what the fuck is wrong with you starting a war in my damn city?"

"Jamila, they was talking about killing you."

"They talk about killing me every fucking day, Symone, and I'm still fucking here ten toes down. And Lorenzo, what the fuck was you thinking about going to the Bronx by yourself. You was the fucking acting Don over the family. You did what you told me not to do and almost got yourself killed. But to put the icing on the fucking cake, Detective Boatman was shot two times in the head and three times in the chest then set on fire. You know what that's called, Symone? A fucking FBI investigation! He was a fucking cop. If you kill a cop, get rid of the damn body. Symone, you don't think you should have called me to tell me what was going on in my city?"

"Jamila, I was taking care of it."

"How, Symone? With a fucking body count?" yelled Jamila, outraged. "Four dead bodies belong to the Scott family. How many of ours is dead? *Six.* I saw six empty seats out there tonight—*six* fucking chairs, Symone! The only smart thing you did was, kill him in front of one of Paul businesses. Symone, why you think I never had Crystal's hands dirty?"

"I don't know," replied Symone.

"Just in case things got hot, nothing will fall back on her. Now she has to play her cards closer than ever before. When they pull Boatman's phone record—and they will—they will see she called him, then what? Lorenzo, you are not hundred percent, so you need to go on a vacation for the next few months. I don't want to see you in the city at all, Lorenzo."

"Yes."

"Try being gone seven months. Don't say nothing, just do it. Symone, you will take his place as my number two until he gets back. Do I make myself clear to both of you?"

"Yes."

"Go. Just know I love you too, and I only want the best for you."

Chapter 15

Jamila had been watching the news about Detective Boatman's murder for three days now. She was looking at the interview with Chief Tadem when her phone went off.

"Hello, Jamila. It's Crystal."

"Hey, are you okay?"

"No, we need to talk. Can you meet me somewhere now?"

"Sure, Crystal, meet me where I make the drop every month," replied Jamila.

"Okay, I'll be there in twenty minutes."

"Okay, I'll see you there." Jamila looked thoughtful as she said to herself: "Something ain't right. I can hear it in Crystal's voice, something got her shook up." Jamila walked to the front lobby, and saw Masi sitting down by the front door.

"Masi, get my car and come on. We need to take a ride."

It took Jamila thirty-five minutes to make it to the drop spot. She saw Crystal as she walked across the street to the limo. Masi got out to open the door for her before he got back in.

"Hey, Crystal, why are you all shook up?" asked Jamila.

"These pictures, Jamila, they just came across my desk, look at them."

Jamila looked at the pictures of her standing over bodies. She remembered that night she killed both of them.

"Where did they come from?"

"Detective Boatman had them on a flash drive. The FBI found it in his house in a safe with millions of dollars."

"How long before they come for me?"

"Two—maybe three—days."

"Okay, let me make some calls. Thank you, Crystal."

"No problem, Jamila, please be safe."

"I will, I promise. Crystal, can I keep these pictures?"

"Yea, you can."

Watching Crystal get out the limo, she looked at Masi and handed him the pictures. Then she picked up the phone and let it ring in her ear until she heard a voice on the other end say: "Attorney office of Christian Williams—"

"How may I help you?"

"May I speak with Attorney Williams, please?"

"I'm sorry, he's presently in a meeting. Would you like to leave a message?"

"Yes, can you tell him to call Jamila LaCross back as soon as possible, please?"

"Wait, hold on, Mrs. LaCross, I think he wants to take this call."

Masi handed back the pictures to Jamila.

"Hello, Mrs. LaCross, what a surprise! I don't know if you calling to get your money back and tell me I'm fired," Christian Williams laughed into the phone.

Jamila let out a light laugh, "No, I'm calling because I need to have a sit-down with you today."

"Okay, this must be big. I been working for you for five years and this is the first time me meeting you. I'm in my office now."

"I'll be there in twenty minutes, I'm on my way."

Jamila walked into Christian Williams' office. He was at the front desk waiting on her.

"Mrs. LaCross, it's good to finally meet you, please follow me to my office."

Jamila took a seat in front of his desk as Masi stood next to his office door.

"So, Mrs. LaCross, what brings you here today?"

"Mr. Williams, I'm in a jam," said Jamila.

"Well, it's nothing I can't handle. I'm known to pull a card out my hat in a tough game."

"Well, I think you need to play with the jokers in this game."

"Okay, tell me what you got?"

Jamila handed him the pictures.

"Take a look at these."

"How did you get these?"

"I have a lot of friends," replied Jamila.

"Damn, now this is a tough game, Mrs. LaCross. They probably are looking for you right now."

"What should I do?"

"First question, how long ago did this happen?"

"About five years back."

"Do you still have the guns?"

"No," said Jamila.

"Okay, look, go handle whatever you need to handle. They are going to lock you up and you might not get a bond just because it's you. Mrs. LaCross, this is going to be big. I'll call you when I'm ready for you to come out of hiding."

"How much is this going to cost me?" asked Jamila.

"You been paying me for the last five years, every month. It's paid for, Mrs. LaCross."

Jamila got up and looked at Mr. Williams. She nodded and turned around, walking out the office.

"Masi, you and the driver—drop me off at my house and go back to *Jelani's* and tell Lorenzo what's going on. Okay?"

"Sure, I will, Mrs. LaCross."

Barely twenty minutes after Jamila got to her house, she saw blue and red lights coming down her driveway. The police were received by her front gate security team. She walked out her back door to a path she had made just in case something like this happened. It took Jamila five minutes to get to her car. She reached the end of the path, got in the car and drove off. She stopped at the top of the hill to see the police raid her house. She was in Paris by 8 o'clock that night, looking at her picture all over the news. Jamila picked up the phone and called Symone.

"Hello."

"Jamila, are you alright?"

"I told you a lot might come from what you did."

"I'm so sorry, I am."

"Symone, we don't have time to be sorry, we have to find a way to fix this. Get with Crystal and see who is handling this case. Besides the murder, what they got on me. I don't want Lorenzo to know nothing right now. You are the head of the family as of right now."

"Where are you at, Jamila?" asked Symone.

"That's not important, what matters is that I'm okay. Now go do what I need you to get done."

"I'm on it now, sis."

"Good, I'll call you in a few days—if not sooner."

"I love you, Jamila."

"I love you more, Symone."

Symone hung up the phone right when her front door was kicked in. "Freeze, don't fucking move."

"What the fuck is going on?" asked Symone, stunned.

"Hands where I can see them."

Symone put her hands in the air.

"We have a search warrant for Jamila LaCross."

"Okay, but this is my house."

"You need to read your deed, it's in her names."

"Clear, clear, she's not in here."

"Okay, have you seen Jamila LaCross?"

"What the fuck kind of question is that?" stated Symone.

"I just heard your men say *clear*. So there's the door, officers, or do I need an attorney?"

"If you are hiding a killer, you might need one."

"She's not here and the door is that way, cop."

"We will see you soon, Symone LaCross."

"Not if I see you first, cop."

"You know I might just want to stay here and go through all your things you have here."

"No, your piece of paper says warrant for a body, and that body is not here. So, you and your team can leave or I can call my attorney on this phone. Just give me five minutes."

"I can't wait to see your face when Jamila gets life in prison."

"The door, cop."

He smiled as he walked out.

"So, what now, sir? You think she knows where Jamila at?"

"No, Jamila's too smart to let anyone know where she at?"

"I don't know how she let herself get caught on camera standing over two dead bodies, sir."

"You know what they say, *you win some you lose some.* You can't win every hand that you are dealt."

***

"Paul, you see the news?"

"Yea, Joe, I did and I think I will have a drink to that."

"It looks like Detective Boatman was of better use to us dead than alive. The LaCross family might just got that inch we been waiting for, Joe."

"While Jamila is on the run, do you want us to go after everyone else in the LaCross family—starting with her sister?"

"No, Joe, they are hot right now. The FBI and everyone else is watching that family until they get Jamila. I don't want nothing falling back on us."

"When it rains, it pours. Let's just hope that Jamila don't have an umbrella, Paul."

"Joe, one thing I can say about Jamila—she don't run from a storm because she knows how to dance in the rain."

"What about Symone, Paul?"

"Symone trying to make a name for herself. She kills with no understanding and that's going to be her downfall, Joe."

SAYNOMORE

Chapter 16

Symone picked up the phone and called Slim Boogie.

"Hello."

"Slim, where you at?"

"I'm at *Destiny's*"

"Okay, I'm coming to get you. I'll be there in five minutes. I'm driving the black Toyota."

"Okay, I'll be out front waiting on you," said Slim.

"Come out front, I'm pulling up now."

"Okay, I see you. Damn, it's raining hard as fuck out here."

Slim ran and jumped in Symone's car."

"You good, Symone?"

"No, I'm not, I'm deep in thoughts. Jamila on the run from the police, and we are still at war. Lorenzo is gone. Slim, I don't want to let my sister down. Yesterday the police kicked in my door, and they might start going to all the other businesses. We don't need that."

"Symone, you might not like what I'm about to say, but Jamila might need to turn herself in to save the family."

"I know, Slim, I know and Jamila told me not to do that shit and I still killed his ass."

"Symone, your phone is going off."

"Hello."

"Hey, how you holding up?"

"I'm good. The police ran in my house yesterday looking for you right after we hung up the phone."

"Okay, I knew that was going to happen, Symone, who are you around right now?" asked Jamila.

"Slim Boogie."

"Okay. Look, I talked to the attorney. I'm turning myself in tomorrow. You have the family meet me at *Jelani's*. It started there; it's going to end there."

"You sure you want to do that, Jamila?"

"I don't have a choice, Symone, in this matter."

"Damn, this is my fault," said Symone.

"Don't say another word in that car, it might be bugged. I'll see you tomorrow."

"I love you, sis."

"I love you more. Tell Slim I said what's up."

"He can hear you."

"I'm here for you, Jamila," said Slim.

"Thanks, Slim, I will see you too tomorrow."

Symone hung up, called Muscle and told him to have everyone meet her at *Jelani's* the next day by 11:30 a.m.

"Symone, with all this going on, you still want the city painted red?"

"Like ketchup! He who fucks with the LaCross family is bound to end up in the belly of the beast."

Chapter 17

It was 5:30 that morning when Jamila's plane landed. She took a cab to *Jelani's*, and went in through the back entrance to her office. She walked into her bird cage inside of the office no one knew about. She made all the calls she needed to make, and then she called Mr. Williams who told her he will be there at 1 p.m. Jamila watched in the camera as Symone entered her office. She had ordered up eight bottles of wine and everything you can think of— from seafood to soul food. There were forty-four seats at the table. Jamila stayed in her office, sending emails out and closing up all loose ends. It was 11:45 when Jamila saw all the members of the LaCross family coming in. She smiled to herself. By twelve noon, everyone was sitting at the table, except for Jamila and Lorenzo. No one saw Jamila when she emerged. She walked up to the glass table and took her seat. She looked at everyone and said: "Let's pray over our meal that Symone put together for us. Symone, would you do the honors if you don't mind?"

Everyone held hands and lowered their heads as Symone spoke.

"Heavenly father, we pray in the name and blood of our Lord and Savior, Jesus Christ, and we thank you for this meal we are about to eat. We thank you for our family, loved ones and years and the blessings you have poured down on us. We thank you in the name of your son—Jesus Christ. Amen."

Jamila stood up. "Everyone, please let's eat."

Seeing that they'd started eating, Jamila continued: "As of right now, everyone knows the police are looking for me. The reason we are here is because I'm turning myself in today. Symone will run the family and you will give her the same loyalty you gave me over the years. I don't know how long I will be gone for or if I can get a bail, but I will not allow what took me over nine years to build up to fall down over me. I love you all. We are the strongest Mafia family in NYC. We stand tall no matter what. What we got here came from love, loyalty, respect and trust. Before she could say another word, Mr. Williams walked in the office—led by KT.

"Mr. Williams, please have a drink with me."

"Sure, Mrs. LaCross."

"So, tell me, Mr. Williams, how is it looking?" asked Jamila.

"Mrs. LaCross, I pulled a lot of strings and called in for a lot of favors. The best I could do is five years and five million dollars donated to the *Stop The Crime Foundation*. And I'm working on you doing two years in prison and three years' probation. That's not guaranteed, though."

"So, when do I have to turn myself in? Does it have to be today?" asked Jamila.

"Today, this is a high-profile case. I have local news teams out waiting on you right now to come outside. Let's get this over with."

Symone had tears in her eyes as she hugged Jamila.

"Symone, it's only five years at the most. I need you to make the family stronger than ever. Keep doing business with Oso. Trust me—he will be in touch with you. I emailed him. I love you. Don't let me down."

That's when Mr. Williams got the phone call that they were waiting on him to bring Jamila downstairs. Jamila looked at her family one more time, walked to the rail and looked down. It had to be over a hundred and fifty people down there. She looked at Chief Tadem and Detective Boatman's partner dead in the eyes, as she made her way downstairs. She looked like a true queen. There were pictures being snapped as she walked downstairs. When she made it to the lobby, Detective Green walked up to her.

"I've been waiting years for this day, and it's an honor for me to put these cuffs on you."

When the Detective put the cuffs on her, Symone said, "Remember, I'm still out here, Detective."

He didn't pay Symone no mind. People took pictures of Jamila being walked out and put in the police truck.

Symone watched as they drove off. She walked in the restaurant with Mr. Williams and closed the door. She looked around. "Everyone, have a seat. There is going to be more heat on us than ever before from the cop killing to the war with the Scott family to our Queen being locked up. We need to move like shadows."

"Symone, what about Lorenzo?"

"Slim, Jamila wants him out the picture," said Symone.

"Mr. Williams, what's next for Jamila?"

"Jamila should have a court date next week. I got her the five years plus the five million dollars she has to donate. I'll try and see if I can get her the two years in prison and three on paper. But then again, I'm not making any promises."

"Okay. So, when can I see her, Mr. Williams?" asked Symone.

"Now that's up to the jail, but I'll see what I can do. Give me a few days and if you need me, Symone, here is my card."

"Thank you, Mr. Williams, I'll be in touch."

"Take care, Symone."

"You too, Mr. Williams."

***

Detective Green looked at Jamila staring out the window as they drove to the jail.

"So the Queen of NYC in handcuffs in the back of a police truck! How does it feel knowing you are going to prison?"

Jamila ain't say a word. She just smiled at the detective as he drove her to the jail. Once at the jail, Detective Green looked at her. "Your five-star hotel awaits you."

"Detective, how does it feel knowing you are an overweight fat pig who only makes about forty-five thousand dollars a year? The chain on my neck cost more than what you made your life out to be. Wait, let me take that back—what your mother's life, your father's life and yours is. My chain cost more than all three of ya lives together." After her parting shot, Jamila had a self-satisfied smirk on her face.

Scowling, Detective Green opened his truck door and slammed it before opening Jamila's door.

"Get out, murderer!"

When Jamila got out, all eyes were on her. She looked around and then was taken to get finger-printed and to change out. No sooner had Jamila sat down than an officer called her name: "Jamila LaCross!"

As she walked up to the desk, she looked at the rookie, eye-balling her distastefully.

"Here is a bag—you need to put all your jewelry in this bag so I can tag it, and you need to go over there where that trash can is and take them fake nails off. There is a fingernail clipper over there. And if that's weave, you need to go over there and have a seat and take it out."

Jamila looked at her before speaking with a smile on her face.

"My hair is real. So are my nails, as well as my jewelry. So I don't need your fingernail clippers by the trash can."

"I don't remember me asking you whether your jewelry was real. I said put it in the bag and I done saw lace wigs before."

"I have too and nappy ponytails. By the way, what's that you have on your head? Horsehair? No, that's not horse hair. That's plastic—two dollars, maybe three dollars at the most—Dollar Store special."

"I don't know who you think you are, but you don't want me to walk around this desk."

"And do what when you walk around the desk?" replied Jamila. "You had better play safe, baby, this is not the ride you want to take."

"You got me fucked up, inmate."

"Nicole, can I have a word with you now?"

"Yes, Captain, here I come."

Jamila just looked as she walked in the back.

"Yea, Captain," replied Nicole.

"Do you know who that is, Nicole?"

"Someone who is about to get my foot put in her ass!"

"That is Jamila LaCross. She is the head of the LaCross family. She is known for having people killed or killing them herself. That woman will kill you and have everything around you killed. Here, read this, it's all over the newspaper."

Nicole looked at the picture of Jamila on the front of the paper.

"Captain, I didn't know."

"Now you do. I will take care of her from here on out, take your fifteen-minute break."

"Hello, I'm sorry for my officer's behavior. I'm Captain Jones and I will be taking care of booking you, and placing all of your property up."

"Thank you, Captain Jones, but where is Nicole? We were just becoming friends."

"I don't think she wants to be the kind of friend you had in mind for her."

Jamila couldn't help but laugh.

"Mrs. LaCross, I know who you are and I can't put you in population," said Captain.

"I'm not going into PC. So, yes, you can. I will be just fine, I promise you that."

"Okay, I'll take your word."

It was an hour and a half when Jamila made it to cell block. She was assigned to *Cell 120*. When she walked in, there was a white female writing a letter on the desk.

"Hello, my name is Amber."

Jamila placed her things down on the desk.

"Hey, my name is Jamila."

"I know, they been talking about you all day in here," said Amber.

"Who has?" asked Jamila.

"Everyone."

"So, Amber, give me the rundown on everything in here."

"Okay. Come on, let's go to the table."

As they sat down, Amber pointed to a table across the room.

"You see that table over there—them girls call themselves CBA, *Cranks Bitches Around*. And over there you have that *Northside Misses*, and over there you have the RKB."

"RKB, Amber?"

"Yea, Jamila—*Real Killer Bitches*. And you have the *White Supremist Girls* and the *Migo Girls* over there."

"So, what are you a part of?"

"I'm just me—that's all," said Amber.

"So, you standing alone?" said Jamila, curious.

"Yea, I have been for the last two years."

"So why you locked up?"

"Drug case. It was my ex-boyfriend's drugs. When the door was kicked in, he got away, but I was in the shower. So they put everything on me because I wouldn't give him up."

"Loyalty. I like that in people. So where is he at now?"

"I ain't heard from him in two years since I been in here. You know one of the CBA girls said you killed her baby father—Ace."

"Which one?" asked Jamila.

"The one with the ponytail sitting at the table."

"What's her name?"

"Rebecca."

"Okay. Come on, let's go back in our cell."

"So how do it feel knowing you can have anything and get away with anything?" asked Amber.

"I can't do whatever I want. Look where I'm at now, sitting there with you. Amber, how old are you?"

"I'm twenty-six years old."

"You are the same age as my little sister. Do you have family out there?"

"No, it's just me and my brother and he's locked up doing ten years on an armed robbery case. He's been locked up six years now."

"How long does he have?" asked Jamila.

"Ten years to the door."

"So how long do you have till you parole out?"

"A few years."

"Well, it looks like we are going to be here for a very long time together. Amber, I'm tired, so I'm going to close my eyes for a little while."

"Okay, I will wake you up for dinner."

"Thanks."

***

"So, Rebecca, what you want to do to that bitch in here now?"

"We going to pull up when the time is right and let her know shit is real, Black."

"I like the sound of that."

"Yea, because ain't no way she going to be up in here thinking shit is sweet after she killed my nigga that way. Her time is coming. Come on, let's get ready for chow."

SAYNOMORE

Chapter 18

"Symone, don't look like that, shit is going to be cool."

"I'm good, Slim Boogie, I just got a lot of shit on my mind."

"I feel you, Symone, but I promise you Red Invee is going to be just fine, she's tough like Barbie."

"I'll go see her next week. So, hear me out, I'm running *Jelani's*, Slim. You got *Passions*. I want Muscle to watch over *Destiny's*, and Masi has the waste plant. These are our biggest money makers. The Scott family is going to try us because they think we are weak, but that's not the case. I want two men at each door and two walking around and one watching the cameras."

"Okay, I'll get on that right away. So what about the six empty seats we have?"

"I almost forgot about that, Slim."

"Well, I have a man. He's big as fuck and is a real killer. They call him Iceman. And his homie name is Pistol Pete."

"Okay, bring them to meet me and we will take it from there, but right now I want eyes everywhere till the Queen is out. This is how it's going to be 24/7. I want KT picking up all the deposits from now on. Tell him I said he should make up four new routes and I'm stressing this, *shoot first and ask questions later*. And Slim, we are not thugs so don't start dressing like one, and let that be known as well."

Slim got up and walked out of Jamila's office. Symone read a plaque that was hanging on Jamila's office wall that said:

"When you get into a tight place and everything goes against you till it seems as though you could not hold on a minute longer, never give up then; for that is just the place and time that the tide will turn."

She read it a few more times before walking off.

***

"It's time for dinner, Jamila."

"How long was I asleep for?"

"About three hours."

"So where we go for dinner?" asked Jamila.

"Follow me."

All eyes were on Jamila when she walked through the halls. Once Jamila saw the food that was served on the trays, she gave her food to Amber. She saw the CBA girls looking at her from the corner of her eyes. Jamila said to herself she was going to pull up on them the first chance she gets. When she was leaving the mess hall, she saw the CBA girls looking at her. That's when she knew they were going to try and make a move.

"Amber, hear me out. I don't want you involved, but I think the CBA girls are going to try something, so I'm going to walk in front of you so you don't get hurt."

"No. Fuck that, Jamila, you are my roommate, so we are going to confront them together."

"If that's what you want."

Once they reached the top of the steps, Jamila asked Amber whether she had a knife or something.

"Yea," Amber replied.

"Where is it at?" asked Jamila.

"Let me get it, hold on. Here you go."

"We're going to get them before they come get us. Where do you think they are at, Amber?"

"In the bathroom, smoking."

"Yea, come on. Let's go see what they talking about."

***

"Yo, Rebecca, what we going to do? What's up with this bitch?"

"I just want her to feel our presence, that's all for now."

Rebecca was sitting on the sink, smoking, when the door opened up. They looked at Jamila and Amber in the doorway. Jamila walked up to Rebecca.

"Do we have a fucking problem, bitch?" said Jamila.

"Bitch, you know we got a fucking problem."

"I was hoping you said that."

It was four CBA girls against Jamila and Amber when Rebecca got off the sink she was sitting on. When the door opened up to the bathroom, four *Northside Misses* came in the bathroom. Rebecca looked at them.

"Yo, this ain't got nothing to do with ya."

"You're right, but we want to make sure the Queen of the city gets a heads up."

Jamila looked at them, then she handed her knife to Amber and put her hair in a ponytail. Rebecca handed her own knife to one of her girls, and walked up to Jamila.

"Bitch, you going to remember this day."

"I sure am," said Jamila then punched Rebecca in the face. Rebecca took two steps back. Jamila rushed her and smacked her in the face with her elbow. Rebecca dropped down to the floor on one knee. Jamila grabbed her by the head with both hands and kneed her dead in the face. Rebecca fell backwards on the floor with blood coming from her nose.

"You said I was going to remember this day, right, bitch?" said Jamila.

While Rebecca was on the floor, Jamila walked up to her. Rebecca kicked her in the stomach, making her take two steps back. Rebecca jumped off the floor, swinging at Jamila. Jamila ducked and grabbed Rebecca's hair by the back of her head, slamming her head into the sink, busting her eye open. She watched as Rebecca fell to the floor again. She got on top of her, punching her in the face nonstop. Blood was splattering everywhere from the impact of Jamila's punches. Jamila grabbed Rebecca's head there and then and started slamming it into the floor.

"Remember what, bitch? Tell me, tell me!"

Amber ran and grabbed Jamila off of Rebecca. Jamila scowled at Rebecca, then walked up to her and kicked her three more times in the face.

"Bitch, next time I'll make sure you and your baby daddy be holding hands again with that bastard ass child of yours."

"Jamila, come on before the CO's come in here."

Jamila and Amber walked out with the *Northside Misses* along-side them. They went to Jamila's cell.

"I don't know ya, but thanks for pulling up," said Jamila.

"No problem, we knew they was going to try you, but we wanted to see what ya do first. And when we saw you pull up. We knew you was going to handle that issue. So we wanted to make sure you ain't got jumped by them dirty bitches."

"Yea, I know they was going to try something by the way they was moving, so I just wanted to beat them to it."

"We respect that, Jamila, how you pulled up."

At that moment, they heard, "Lockdown for count!"

"Queen, you know where we are at if you need us."

"I got you, Lady Misses."

"Jamila, I did not know you could fight like that."

Jamila gave a short laugh. "And why is that, Amber?"

"You have long pretty hair, long fingernails and you don't even have no marks on your face. You don't look like a fighter type."

"Amber, you don't never suppose' to look like what you really are. NYC calls me an angel, but behind my back they call me the mother of death. But the one question is, do I look like a killer?"

"No, you don't."

"And that's my point, Amber."

"Well, your first day in lock up, you done stomped a bitch the fuck out and got a name for yourself."

"Yea, what a first day!"

Chapter 19

One Week Later—

"So, who is that girl over there?" asked Jamila.

"That's Ms. Rose playing chess. She's the best in here by far. You play chess?"

'Yea, I do."

"If you want to play, she will play you. She's really a nice lady."

"No, I might play her some other time."

Jamila was looking out the doorway to her cell when she heard her name.

"Jamila LaCross."

"Yea."

"Get ready, you have an attorney visit."

"I'll be back, Amber, let's see what my attorney has to tell me."

"You might have some good news—you never know, Jamila," said Amber, smiling.

"I bet," replied Jamila as she walked toward the officer.

"Which way, officer?"

"The door to the right over there—your attorney is in there waiting for you now," said the officer.

When Jamila opened the door, Symone was in there waiting for her. She had her back to Jamila, looking out the window. Symone had on an all-black dress with a black coat that matched her dress. She wore a pair of black shoes with three-inch heels, and her hair was in a ponytail. She was wearing some silver earrings and a matching chain. When Symone turned around, Jamila broke into laugh.

"Damn, girl, I ain't know who the hell you was."

"I'm your new attorney, Ms. LaCross," replied Symone, giving Jamila a discreet wink

They both started laughing. Jamila walked up and gave Symone a hug.

"So, Jamila, how you holding up in here?"

"It's not bad at all. I'll make it."

Symone was looking at Jamila's hands.

"What happened to your hands?"

"I ran into Ace's baby mother last week and had to give that bitch some act right."

"Do I have to pay her family a visit?" replied Symone.

"No. Trust me, Symone, I beat da bitch ass real good last week. So, what's happening out there?"

"Nothing. It's quiet for right now, but I got everyone's ears to the ground, and I'm still moving the powder. I have a meeting with Oso next week."

"Okay good. I knew I could put my trust in you. Symone, this is what I need you to do. The mayor is having a ball or a fundraiser, I think, to aid a couple of foundations. Our children are our future, so we need to help raise money for them."

"Okay, what you want me to do, Jamila?"

"Five million dollars to the *Stop The Crime Act*, and three million dollars to the children's foundation. And Symone, let them know it came from the LaCross Foundation. You and one more person should go and get the mayor a gift, his wife too. Get him a diamond watch and his wife a diamond tennis bracelet. Let him know it came from me."

"I will," replied Symone. "I also put two thousand dollars on your books today."

"Thank you!"

"And you should be in court next week to take your plea. Other than that, everything else is good."

"Okay."

"And I will see you this week at court, Mrs. LaCross."

'You are too much, Symone. Thank you."

"I love you, Jamila!"

Symone got up and waved to the CO to come get Jamila.

"I love you too, Symone."

When Jamila walked back to her cell block, she saw Amber playing chess with one of the *Northside Misses*. Jamila walked in her cell and lay down on her bed, thinking how good her little sister is doing right now. *I just hope she keeps it up*, Jamila thought.

***

"Symone, how is she holding up in there?"

"She good. She ran into Ace's baby mother a week ago."

"How that go?"

"She said she beat her ass, Slim."

"Niggas know your sister is not the one to be fucked with at all. So, what now, Symone?"

"Call KT and have him pick up all the deposits so we can get that out the way. And call Muscle and make sure everyone is where they need to be."

"I'm doing that right now."

When Symone pulled up at *Jelani's*, she saw two black cars out front. When she walked in, there were six men and a female waiting on her. Masi walked up to her.

"Symone."

"Yea, Masi, whose cars are parked out front?"

"That's what I was coming to tell you. I only know the female's name and they are here to talk to you."

"What's the female's name?" asked Symone.

"Rose."

That's when the lady walked over to Symone and Masi.

"Excuse me, Symone LaCross?"

"Yes, that is me."

"My name is Rose and these men are my colleagues. We would like to have a word with you."

Symone looked at all of them.

"Okay, please follow me to my office."

Once they made it to her office, Symone walked to the diamond table.

"Please, everyone, have a seat and tell me how I can help you," replied Symone.

"To jump to the point, to our understanding you are the head of the LaCross family in Jamila's absence?"

"Yes, I am, Ms. Rose."

"Ms. LaCross, we have done a lot of business with the LaCross family."

"Ms. Rose, not to be rude or disrespectful, but where is all this going?" asked Symone.

"We just want to make sure everything is running smooth with our business while you are in her place, Symone," replied Ms. Rose.

"Ms. Rose, I will assure you everything is still going to run smooth just the way it has been while I'm in her place."

"That's good to hear, Ms. LaCross, and we will start the construction on the ocean front properties this month. Will you let Jamila know that?"

"I will. Do you have a card, Ms. Rose?"

"Yes, I do, here you go. Just so you know, Symone, me and your sister been in business for over two years now. But funnily enough, Symone, I've never been in here before."

"You haven't? Okay. Please all of you stay for lunch, it's on the house."

"Thank you, Symone, and we will."

Symone picked up the phone and called the waiter to her office so she could usher them to the VIP area. Symone knew who they were when Ms. Rose said, *ocean front properties*; that's why she offered them lunch on the house. They were members of the Temple.

Chapter 20

"Joe, Jamila's locked up. I think it's time we start to rip the LaCross family apart limb by limb." Paul got up from his desk with a smile on his face. That's when his door opened up.

"Mr. Scott, you have a guest outside who wishes to talk to you."

"Who is it?"

"A Mr. Deoblow."

"Let him know I'll be right there."

"I will, sir."

Paul picked up his jacket from the back of the chair and put it on, then looked in the mirror. "Joe, I'll be back in a few."

When Paul walked outside to the lobby, he smiled as he shook Mr. Deoblow's hand.

"Mr. Deoblow, how you doing? It's nice to see you."

"Likewise, Paul. Come take a ride with me. It's beautiful outside."

"Sure, why not?" Paul said as he got in the limo with Deoblow. "So, tell me—what brings you to New York City, Deoblow?"

"I was seeing how our business was going with Red Invee."

"Well, as of right now she is in jail, but I do have someone working on that as we speak."

"So Paul, how long are we talking?" asked Deoblow.

"A few weeks at the most."

"This is my third time to New York City. I really don't know how you Americans do business, but in Mexico we do business differently. If we say we going to get something done, we get it done in a few days, a week at the most."

"Mr. Deoblow, are you saying I can't get what I said done?" asked Paul.

"What I am saying, Mr. Scott, is that my patience is running low. I gave you one million dollars up front already."

"I understand, but Jamila is not an easy target. I put my family at war just to get the job done."

"Mr. Scott, my friend, you said it was a piece of cake. That's how you Americans say it, right? And I trusted your word in this matter."

"I stand on my word, and I honor my word at all times."

"I sure hope so for the sake of our friendship. I will be in New York City for three more days. I'm staying at the Hilton hotel in Manhattan."

Paul nodded. "I'm just watching how the LaCross family moves. I want to know how they got so powerful in such a short time."

"Mr. Scott, if Jamila is the Queen Don, that makes Symone the Princess of the city."

"Symone is on my list to kill as well, Mr. Deoblow."

"Well, Paul, do what must be done then. I will be in touch."

"Take care, Mr. Deoblow."

Paul stepped out of the limo, and watched it pull off. *I should just kill that fucker and get a free million. I need a fucking drink.*

Joe came outside to meet Paul. "Is everything alright?"

"No, I don't know who the fuck that Mexican think he is, but I'll kill all them motherfuckers."

"Paul, are you going to the mayor's fundraiser tonight?"

"No, I have other affairs to attend to."

***

"Symone, what time you want to meet up?"

"How about between six-thirty and seven p.m.? I don't want to be too early or too late."

"Okay. I'll see you in a few hours, Symone."

"Slim, make sure you are dressed up. There are going to be a lot of very important people there tonight—the mayor, the Chief of police, judges, DA's etc. You get what I'm saying?"

"Symone, I got you."

"Cool. I'ma have a car pick us up at *Jelani's*, so make sure you are there by five-thirty p.m."

"I'll be there."

That afternoon, Symone had a hair appointment at Smiley's at 3:30. She went and got her nails and toes done already. She had her fingernails painted red with a black L on her middle finger and her big toe. It was 3 o'clock when she pulled up at Smiley's, though.

"Hey, Smiley"

"Hey, girl. I started to think you ain't know us no more down here."

"Smiley, stop that. How could I forget about you?"

"You know I'm just kidding, child. So, tell me, what am I doing for you today?"

"I have to go to the mayor's fundraiser, so I have to look fabulous," said Symone.

"I got you. What time you have to be there?"

"It starts at eight, but I have to be back at *Jelani's* by six-thirty."

"You will be done way before that. Now let's get you a wash. I saw the news a few weeks ago. Even with handcuffs on, Jamila still looked like the Queen of the city. How is she doing in there?"

"I went to see her. She's good, just waiting to come home. So how are things around here, Smiley?"

"Same shit different day. Guess who I saw a few weeks ago?"

"Who?" replied Symone, curious.

"Your old boo thing—Prince."

Symone cut her eyes at Smiley. "I can't stand that boy."

"I know you can't, and he asked about you."

"And why was that?"

"He saw when Jamila got locked up and I told him you was the head bitch in charge now. Girl, he just dropped his head. But come on, let's get you washed up so you can go show out tonight."

Symone made it home by 4:45 p.m. She put on a red skin-tight dress with an open back, with a slit going up her right thigh and black lines running through her dress. She had a diamond cut in front of her dress, showing off a little cleavage, with a diamond-encrusted dog chain around her neck. She was wearing a pair of beautiful diamond earrings and a gold tennis bracelet. Her hair was pressed down with curls at the tips. She had an open-toe red bottom shoes with the straps around the ankles, completing the ensemble with a black Louis Vuitton bag. When the limo pulled up at *Jelani's*, Slim was in the front. Wearing a pair of Stacy Adams, he had on a black and white suit accompanied by a dark tie, with a coal-black vest and belt. A pair of 2 karat diamond earrings adorned his ears. A white scarf hanging off his shoulders, he wore a low haircut, and a gold Rolex.

"Damn, Slim, you look too handsome."

"No, Symone, you look too damn sexy. What the fuck, girl!"

"Come on, Slim, let's go. I don't want to be late."

***

"You okay, Jamila?" asked Amber.

"Yea, I'm just a little nervous. My sister went to the mayor's ball and fundraiser tonight in my place, and I just hope it goes right tonight."

"What time is it?"

"It starts at eight p.m."

"Hold on, Jamila, I'll be right back."

"Where are you going, Amber?"

"Jamila, come check this out. The mayor's ball is being shot live on Channel 7 news, and the girls are already watching it. It's on in the TV room now."

"Are you for real?" said Jamila.

"Yea. Come on, Jamila."

When Jamila walked in the TV room, everyone was watching the mayor's ball.

***

"Slim, do you see all of these people?"

"Yea, Symone, this is crazy."

When the limo pulled up, cameras swung into action with flashing lights of the pictures being taken of her and Slim as they got out the limo. Symone looked around, and was waving at the people taking the pictures. She and Slim were the center of attention.

***

Jamila was looking at Symone on TV. She looked like the Queen of the city.

"Jamila, that's your little sister?"

"Yea and her right-hand man—Slim Boogie."

"Shit! Jamila, she is rocking that dress fo' real."

Jamila smiled. "She is, Amber. Slim is looking like a real mobster, I tell you."

"He is fly, girl. I was just saying that to myself. Jamila, until you get out, I think we are looking at the new Queen and King of NYC."

Jamila ain't say a word. She was watching Symone's every move from the way she walked to the way she smiled, even to the way she waved at people. Symone walked with confidence. She was bold. She was dangerous, and New York City knew at that moment she was the reigning Queen.

"Shit, shit, shit!"

"What is it, Jamila?" asked Amber.

"I forgot to tell her she needs to make a speech."

***

"Everyone, take your seats please," said the compere. Symone sat at the LaCross table.

"Everyone, the mayor is about to make his speech," the compere added.

That's when one of the directors walked up to Symone.

"Ms. LaCross, after the mayor makes his speech, you are up. Be ready when this red light comes on."

"Wait, I did not know I was making a speech."

"Yea, you are."

"Okay, I'll be ready," said Symone.

"Well, Symone, you have about five minutes to make something up because the mayor is going on stage now."

"Ladies and gentlemen, New York City Mayor Cray." Everyone started clapping when they saw the mayor go on stage.

"I done seen a lot of crime growing up in NYC. Just like there is a lot of crime in other major cities, murders, drugs, rape, and robbery, but we are going to work on making New York City better. Crime happens, and that's just a cold fact of life, and you know what's another fact? I love New York City. I think it's the best city in the world. In the last six years, crime has increased by ten percent. We need these numbers to drop to zero. That's the point of this ball tonight. We want a school system to help our children grow into adults with careers—not thugs with criminal minds. So, tonight, let's help New York City be a better city for children to grow up in. A brighter city with a brighter future for our children."

Everyone gave the mayor a standing ovation. The light started to blink at Simon's table to let her know that she was up next to make her speech.

"Please, everyone, give a hand to Symone LaCross."

Symone got up to make her speech. Jamila was watching quietly as Symone walked on stage.

"Good evening, everyone. As Mayor Cray just said, NYC is the greatest city in the world, and I am proud to be called a New Yorker. I grew up in Southside Jamaica—Queens—but my mother and her mother grew up in the Bronx. So, NY has a great deal of my family history in it. I am here taking my beautiful sister Jamila LaCross place tonight because she could not be here tonight. But she did tell me to say that she is a proud New Yorker, and on behalf of the LaCross Foundation she is donating three million dollars to the school system. Mayor Cray, can you please come receive this check?"

"She is doing good, Jamila."

"No, she is doing great, Amber."

"Thank you!" Mayor Cray held up the check and smiled

"But that's not all, Mayor Cray. The LaCross Foundation is also donating five million dollars to the *Stop The Crime Act* in NYC to help our law enforcement men and women to be safe on the job with better crime fighting tools, and we have one more donation. It's to the group home known as a *Bright Future For A Better Tomorrow*. We are donating one million dollars."

"On behalf of New York City," said the mayor, "thank you to the LaCross Foundation."

Everyone started to clap. The mayor and Symone took three pictures on stage before going back to their seats. It was already 9:30 p.m., and everyone was eating. The mayor was at the table with Symone and Slim.

"Symone, that was very nice of you to donate all that money to NYC."

"It was very nice for what you did for my sister, Mayor. That's our way of saying thank you. She told me to give you this—"

Symone handed the diamond Rolex watch and his wife the diamond-encrusted tennis bracelet.

"Symone, this is beautiful, tell your sister we said *thank you*. Now, if you will excuse us, we have to go take pictures with the rest of the guests. Please enjoy the rest of your evening."

"I understand. Take care, Mayor."

"You too, Symone."

***

"You good now, Jamila, your sister held it down."

"Yea, she did her thing, I can say."

"She learned a lot from you, Jamila."

"I sure hope so."

"Now come on, Jamila, you owe me my rematch in chess," said Amber.

"Amber, I'm not going to let you beat me."

"We will see."

They both started laughing.

***

"Symone, tonight was crazy. I still can't believe we had the mayor sitting at our table."

"Trust me, Slim. I couldn't believe it at all, facts! Hold on, Muscle's calling me."

"Hello."

"Yo, Symone, we have two members from the Scott family that's been parked up the block from *Destiny's* for the last three hours. I was going to make a move on them, but I wanted to talk to you first since you said the war with them is over."

"You sure it's them?"

"Yea, they been sitting in a black Ford all night."

"Okay, I'm on my way to the hotel now."

"What happened, Symone?" asked Slim.

"You have two of the Scott family members sitting in the front of *Destiny's*. They been there for three hours."

When the limo pulled up, Symone had the driver stop beside the black Ford. She rolled down the window so they could see her, then she opened the door to let them get in.

"Hello, gentlemen."

"Symone."

"So can you tell me the reason you been parked down the street from my hotel for the last the hours?"

"It's a road. What? We can't be parked on it?"

"Cut the bullshit, why are you over here?" asked Symone.

"Here's the deal, our boss wants peace, you want peace. So to keep it that way, he wants five percent of all your businesses and he wants to open up a spot in Queens."

Symone looked at him like he was crazy. "Are you for real?"

"Yes, dead ass."

"And if I say no?"

"Then you know where we go from here."

"I see. I'm guessing since my sister is locked up, Paul thinks I'm weak."

"Look at it this way, Symone, it's just good business."

"You right. It's good business. Can you call Paul for me please, if you don't mind?" said Symone.

"Sure, hold on."

Symone watched as he pulled his phone out and called Paul.

"Hey, boss, she wants to talk to you."

"Put her on the phone," said Paul.

"Here you go."

Symone took the phone from him.

"Hello, I just want to make sure what your men are saying is true that you want five percent of my business and open up a night spot. So I guess you feel you can sell on my side of town?"

"That's right, it's time we do some new business with each other."

"And Paul, where is all this coming from?" asked Symone.

"Look, ain't no nigga going to run shit without paying no dues and if you don't like what I'm saying, I can have someone go talk to the monkey in the cage already."

"Paul, I want you to hear me very clearly," Symone pulled out her gun. Before Paul's men saw it coming, she shot both of them in the head, pushing their brains on the floor of the limo, killing them on the spot. Symone yelled to Paul in the phone, "You're next, pussy." Then she hung the phone up. Symone looked down at Paul's men and spat on their dead bodies.

"Slim, call Muscle and have him come outside now. Driver—"

"I know, Ms. LaCross—to the waste plant."

"Yea—and take Muscle with you," said Symone.

When Muscle got in the limo, he saw the dead bodies.

"I'm guessing guns up again."

Symone nodded. "Yea, get rid of these two, clean the limo up and bring it to our friends in New Jersey. Kent, get another limo and pick me up in two hours from here."

Deoblow was across the street, watching everything.

"Deoblow, did you just see that?"

"Yea, I saw the flash through the tinted windows. They should have known she was going to kill them. She ain't think twice about pulling the trigger. That's why the LaCross family is so feared. They not afraid to shoot on sight."

"So, you want me to follow the limo to see where they are taking the bodies?"

"No, I want to watch her some more."

Symone stepped out of the limo and walked across the street where she had three men waiting on her at.

"Deoblow, is that Symone?"

"Yes, Carlito, that is the Queen of New York City's little sister."

"She don't look like a killer at all."

"But you see she is a cold-hearted killer. Don't let the innocent look fool you. Let me call our good friend—Paul."

***

Paul looked at the phone as he lit his cigar.

"What she say, Paul?"

"Joe, she just killed both of them. I want blood for this. I want that bitch dead by the end of next week."

Paul looked to see his phone ringing. He walked over to his desk and picked it up.

"Yea."

"It's Deoblow, Paul, I just wanted to tell you our little angel just sent your men on a trip they will not come back from."

"You must have seen it."

"Yea, I saw it."

Deoblow hung up after he said that. Paul looked at the phone and threw it to the wall, breaking it.

"Joe, I want that bitch dead now."

Chapter 21

"Slim, where you at?"

"I'm at *Passions*."

"Okay. Tomorrow I want you, Muscle and Masi to meet me at *Jelani's* at seven-thirty p.m. and make sure everyone have extra clips and two guns."

"Say no more, Symone, we will be there."

"Slim, I'm at the point where I don't give no fucks no more. Everything we do from here on out—we are going to leave a body count. That's our fucking signature—a kiss of death!"

"I'm on it, Symone."

"Good."

Symone hung up and blew smoke out her mouth, thinking about how she wanted to kill Paul.

***

"Hey, Jamila, you up for a game of chess?"

"No, Amber, I have a lot on my mind right now."

"What's up? Talk to me. What's on your mind?" asked Amber.

"My little sister and how she is holding the family down. She looked so beautiful last night."

"She did, but *beautiful* is an understatement. Did you try and call her last night?"

"Yea, a few times and she ain't pick up," replied Jamila.

"You think something is wrong?"

"I don't know. I'll try back tonight. She did have a long night last night."

"Jamila, can I ask you something?" said Amber.

"Yea, what's up?"

"The life you are living, did you want to live it?"

"To be honest, Amber, I was born into this life and never knew it. My father was showing me this life as a little girl. Do I regret it? *No*. Do I wish I could take a lot of things back? *Yes*. I lost my boyfriend. I been shot and almost got killed three times. And the man who was like my father was killed because of me. The man who I thought loved me tried to kill me, so there's no turning back for me now. My life ends in a black bag, and that will be the ending of my story, Amber."

"So you don't see a happy ever after, Jamila?"

"This is the MOB, Amber. Our death is our happy ever after."

Amber looked at Jamila and ain't say another word. She just nodded and walked out the door.

Chapter 22

Symone watched as everyone sat down in her office. All eyes were on her.

"I'm tired of those muthafuckers thinking I'm someone to play with, so tonight the takeover starts. We are about to go to Joe's penthouse downtown and take what I want with no questions asked. If anybody gets in our way, kill them."

"Symone, do we know how many people he has there with him?"

"No and I don't care who is there with him. Just know when their guns are raising, ours should be blazing. Slim, come on, let's get this over with now. Slim, is KT downstairs?"

"Yea, I saw him downstairs."

"Good, tell him to come on. I want him as the driver just in case we have to get out of there fast."

Symone took the elevator up to the Penthouse when they got to the hotel. Slim, Masi and Muscle took the stairs. She waited for them to call her to let her know they were on the Penthouse floor waiting on her. When Symone made it to the top floor, she got off the elevator. There were two bodyguards standing outside Joe's door. Symone had both her hands behind her back as she walked up to them.

"Hold up, stop right there, who you here to see?" one of the body guards asked her.

"I'm here to see Mr. Joe Scott."

"I don't remember him saying he was expecting more guests."

Both bodyguards started walking to Symone, not realizing who she was. Once they were close enough, Symone pulled both guns out from behind her back and pointed it at them. That's when Slim, Muscle and Masi ran out from behind the staircase, guns in hand.

"The reason you ain't know I was coming is because he wasn't expecting me," said Symone.

"Shit," one of the guards said, as he had Slim's gun to his face.

Masi walked up to one of the guards. "Who is inside with him?"

"Fuck you, nigga."

Masi smiled and smacked him in the head with the gun, dropping him. Muscle pointed the gun at his face once he was on the floor.

"Your turn," Masi said to the other guard, "but this time we are going to pull the trigger. Who is inside with him?"

Shaking his head and closing his eyes, the guard said: "He only have one female in there right now."

Masi took the door key from the bodyguard as they walked back to Joe's penthouse suite. The music was playing so loud that Joe ain't hear them come inside. Slim and Muscle tied up the bodyguards, as Symone and Masi waked to the living area. Symone was looking at Joe getting his dick sucked, laying back on the couch with his eyes closed. Symone walked up to the table and picked up a green apple that was in a fruit basket, and sat down at the table and watched on. Slim and Masi stood behind her, not saying a word.

"Damn, baby, this feels good, keep going. I'm about to cum, don't stop."

Joe placed his hand on top of her head as he was cumming. After Joe came in her mouth, she got up in order to spit it out. That's when she saw Symone. She let out a scream. Slim and Masi pulled their guns out on Joe.

"Bitch, if you don't shut the fuck up, I'll see if you can fly tonight."

Joe tried to pull up his pants, but Masi smacked him in the face, dropping him to the floor. Symone was still eating her apple as she looked at the girl. "What is your name?"

"Candy."

"Listen, Candy, I want you to come over here and sit down very quietly, do you understand me?"

"Yes."

"Good, now come sit down. I would hate to kill you tonight. Good evening, Joe. Shit! I know you feel good tonight now that you got that nut off."

Joe ain't say nothing. He just looked at Symone. Symone took a bite of her green apple and walked to the sliding glass door.

"Joe, you have a beautiful view."

Symone turned around and looked at Joe on the floor with his dick out.

"Masi, let him pick his pants up. I don't want to see that pink worm."

Joe picked his pants up as Masi had his gun pointed at him.

"So, Joe, since the Scott family thinks I'm a weak link, let's talk business. Since Paul sent his men to tell me he wants five percent of all my businesses, I figure I'll start *my* takeover by taking the night spot-casino you have.

"Fuck you! You think you can come up in my penthouse and bully me around! Do you know who the fuck I am?"

Masi kicked him in the face as he was talking, making blood burst from his lip.

"Muscle, come here. This mutherfucker asked me do I know who the fuck he is! He must not know who the fuck I am. Pick this pussy up and throw his ass out them sliding doors. Let's see how far his blood spills when he hit the fucking ground."

Joe resisted, but Slim smacked him in the face with the gun. Muscle grabbed him in a full nelson with his arms over his head as Masi punched him in the face twice, taking the fight out of him. Muscle and Slim dragged him out the sliding glass doors, and hung him upside down from the 26th floor of his penthouse.

"Pick me up, don't drop me, pick me up."

Symone nodded to Muscle and Slim to pull him up. Once back over the rail, Joe started throwing up the instant he hit the floor. Symone looked at him and threw her apple over the rail.

"Joe, where are the deeds at?"

Joe got up, walked her to his safe, opened it up and pulled out three yellow envelopes."

"Joe, now hand me the envelope, please."

Symone looked at them.

"Joe, you also own the *Pay Your Way* strip club. You will sign that over to me too."

Joe looked at Masi's gun in his face as he signed over both

properties to Symone. Joe also had $300,000 in the safe. After bagging the money up, Symone took out $10,000.

"Candy, come here."

"Yes, please don't hurt me, I swear I won't say nothing."

"I believe you, but here is ten thousand dollars for putting that in your mouth, and that still ain't enough for swallowing that shit."

"Joe, remember I did this to you. Now have your shit out of my spots by tomorrow night or I'll see if your ass can fly for real. Tie his ass back up."

Joe just looked at her and his bodyguards. Symone pulled her gun out and shot both guards in the head, killing them, splashing blood everywhere. Then they walked out. KT was waiting on them when they walked out.

"Symone."

"Yea, Slim."

"Why you kill them guards?"

"What did I say before we left? Our signature is our body count. I was dead ass for real. And Slim, don't ever question me again."

Chapter 23

"Move the fuck out the way, move dammit!"

Joe yelled at everyone as he marched into Paul's bar. Paul looked at him.

"What got into you, Joe?"

"You don't know? That nigga Symone walked into my penthouse, hung me upside down twenty-six stories' high and killed two of my bodyguards."

"And she ain't kill you, why?" asked Paul.

"Let me get a drink." Joe poured himself a drink.

"So why she ain't kill you?"

"She made me sign over the casino and the *Pay Your Way* strip club to her last night," said Joe.

"So you telling me this porch monkey took over a million dollar business and you fucking let her?"

"I had no choice. I was hanging from my twenty-sixth-floor deck."

"You know what? I want a meeting here with everyone by one o'clock. We are going to put an end to this nigga."

Joe sat still, a bland expression on his face.

"Joe."

"Yea."

"Get the fuck out and do what I just said. Why are you still sitting here? Bye, bye!"

***

Symone walked into Mr. Williams' office.

"Hello, may I help you?"

"Yes, I'm here to see Mr. Williams."

"And what is your name?"

"Symone LaCross."

"Okay, I will let him know you are here."

"Ms. LaCross, he said you can come on back."

"Symone, how are you doing today?"

"I'm doing good, Mr. Williams."

"So tell me, Symone, what brings you here today."

"I have some things I need you to look over for me."

"Sure, let me see what you got."

Symone passed Mr. Williams the folder.

"Symone, these are the deeds to the casino downtown, and this is the deed to the *Pay Your Way* strip club. This casino brings in over a million dollars a week."

"Mr. Williams, I need you to make sure all my i's are dotted and all my t's crossed."

"Okay, I can do that. I'll get on that right away."

"Thank you and this is for you."

Symone placed a suitcase on his desk. When he opened the suitcase, there was $290,000 dollars in it.

"And what is this for Symone?" asked Mr. Williams.

"A gift from the LaCross family, Mr. Williams."

"Thank you and I'll get on this right away, Symone."

As Symone was walking out of Mr. Williams' office, her phone went off.

"Hello."

You have a collect call from Jamila LaCross, press 1 to accept it. Hold on, your call is being connected.

"Hey, sis."

"What's up, little sis?"

"Nothing, just leaving Mr. Williams' office."

"Is everything okay?" asked Jamila, concerned.

"Yea, just somethings I can't talk with you over the phone about."

"Okay, so I saw you at the mayor's fundraiser. You looked outstanding!"

"You know I had to put on for the family."

"I know," replied Jamila

"So how are you holding up in there?" asked Symone.

"Good, it's really not that bad."

"I forgot to tell you I sent you a food package this week."

"Thank you!" said Jamila.

You have fifteen seconds left on the phone call.

"Symone, the phone is about to hang up. I love you and I'll call you later this week."

"I love you more, big sis."

Symone put the phone in her bag and looked out the window of her limo. She was thinking about the two men that she was about to meet—Iceman and Pistol Pete.

***

Paul looked at everyone sitting around the large table in his office. "We been at war with the LaCross family for over six months now and we are winning. Them niggas are dropping like flies but this cockroach—*Symone*—is a bigger pain in my ass than her sister—Jamila. She just killed two of our guys, and poor old Joe she hung upside down from the 26th floor penthouse deck. So let's pay her back. I want a team to go by *Destiny's* and kill everything you see."

"Why not *Passions* or *Jelani's*?"

"Because she will be waiting on us to strike them, Joe. I want to see dead bodies on the news. I want that place burnt down. She done killed over eight of our family members in the last six months. This is war and—dammit—we will win. We will not end up like the Deniro family or the Lenacci family. That is not how our story ends. I want Symone dead by the end of the week. I don't care who pulls the trigger, just get it done. I want this story on the news. I said what I needed to say. I don't have nothing else to say.

***

KT was smoking his blunt, sitting on the hood of the car, when Muscle pulled up.

"KT, what's good, bro?"

"Shit, Muscle, I just been thinking we been putting in a lot of work, chopping niggas the fuck up, hanging them off of buildings."

"So fucking what! KT, we been getting paid. Facts—big money. We rocking seven thousand-dollar suits, we got the streets on lock."

"Yea, I feel you, homie, real shit. Muscle, we are the goons on the block niggas fear."

"You crazy as fuck, KT, Symone put more work in than us. She stay catching a body. You ain't see the way she killed them niggas the other night eating on a green apple while we hung that nigga off the side of the building. She on her real boss shit. Cutting motherfuckers' ears and fingers off. Check this out, KT, about two weeks ago she calls me to come pick her up. I get there, she gets in my car and lights a *black-n-mild* and gave me an address to go to. It was an old apt building. When we walked inside, she had this dude butt ass naked in a tub tied up. She sat next to the tub and asked him a few questions. The water was blood red. She got up and got two bags of ice and poured them on him. I ain't know what the fuck she had going on. I looked closer, this dude was missing his whole fucking left leg. KT that shit was cut the fuck off. He was shaking. His eyes were pale blue, and so were his lips. KT, she sat there with her legs crossed like everything was cool, smoking a *black-n-mild*."

"Who was he, Muscle?"

"When you see shit like that, you don't ask questions, bro, or you might end up in a fucking tub with one leg. But let me finish. So a doctor of Symone's is standing by the door. Symone ask the nigga in the tub a few more questions, he said he don't know. So, she cut his throat from ear to ear and told the doctor to donate his body parts. Then we walked out of there and she ain't say a word about it no more. That shit still got me fucked up."

Muscle stopped talking when he looked away and saw something strange. "Hey, KT, you see that car that just pulled up over there?"

When KT turned around and looked, he saw guns aimed at him and Muscle.

"Oh shit. Down, down."

Guns shots erupted as *Destiny's* was shot up. KT and Muscle were behind KT's car as the gun fire was coming their way. That's when two Molotov cocktails went flying in the window, setting *Destiny's* front lobby on fire before the assailants peeled off.

"KT, you good?" asked Muscle.

"Yea, damn, call Symone and tell her we got hit."

"Fuck that. Right now, KT, we got to put this fire out."

Three of Symone's men got killed. The hotel was on fire, two guests were shot. Muscle called Symone.

"Yo, Symone, where you at?"

"*Jelani's*, what's up?"

"They just hit *Destiny's* up. Three bodies. Two guests got shot, and they set the hotel on fire, but we put it out before it was too bad."

Symone closed her eyes and rubbed her forehead.

"Muscle, you and KT come to *Jelani's*, and I'll have Slim and Masi come there to take care of it. I want to know what happened."

"We on our way now."

***

"Jamila, you are about to go on your run?"

"Yea, you should come run with me, Amber."

"Jamila, you been asking me to run with you for months now, and the answer is still no."

"When you get older, you are going to wish you have."

"Well, I will cross that path when I get there."

"Yard call, yard call, going out."

"I'll see you when I get back in, Amber," said Jamila.

"Okay. Do enough running for the both of us, Jamila."

"Yea, okay, Amber," Jamila laughed as she walked out.

"Jamila LaCross, come here for a second."

"Sure, what's up, Captain?"

"Come walk outside with me."

"What's going on?" asked Jamila.

"Don't you own that five-star hotel—*Destiny's*?

"Yea, I do."

"You might want to go watch the news. It was shot up and set on fire last night, leaving three people dead and two guests shot."

"Damn, can I go back in, Captain? I have to make a call?"

"Yea, the door is open."

Jamila ran inside and called Symone, but nobody picked up. She tried two more times before going in the TV room to see the news.

Chapter 25

Jamila sat on her bed, waiting for the doors to pop open so she can use the phone to try and call Symone again. That was when the two jail guards came to get her.

"Jamila, you have a visitor who wishes to speak to you, come with us."

Amber looked as they walked Jamila out the cell. Jamila walked in the room where two detectives were waiting on her.

"Jamila LaCross, come in and have a seat."

"No, I will stand if you don't mind. Now can you tell me, what I can do for you?"

"Right now, there is a war on the streets and it's no secret your little sister Symone is running the LaCross family while you are here. And Paul Scott and your sister are at war, and we need to end this war."

"So why you come to see me?" asked Jamila.

"To see if you can help us put an end to this war in NYC."

"You mean tell you what I know?"

"If it can help us stop this war, then *yes*. I need to know what you know."

"You cops, detectives, are too funny. Well, I'm sorry to bust your bubble. I don't know anything, so I'm sorry I can't help you."

Jamila knocked on the door, signaling to the guard that she was ready to leave the room.

"I guess money can buy you freedom—Imagine a female standing over two dead bodies with the gun in her hand and only gets five years in prison," one of the detectives said.

"You are right, detective. That's why I love our justice system. It's the best in the world."

As Jamila walked back to her cell, she knew they ain't have nothing and they needed information, so she had to tell Symone.

***

"Slim, where is KT at?"

"He said he was going to hold *Destiny's* down til' we finish making these drops."

"Okay, Muscle, be on the lookout because right now the Scott family has eyes on us. Masi, shoot first."

"I got you, Symone."

"Slim, what route are we taking?"

"The one KT been taking. He said it beats traffic and it's faster."

Symone watched as they drove down the road in Slim's Hummer. She needed a way to kill Paul before he killed her.

"Slim, how long ya been taking this route?"

"For about three weeks now."

"Slim, stop at the red light."

Symone watched as a garbage truck passed them.

"Muscle, from now on I want you at *Jelani's* with me."

That's when bullets started hitting the Hummer. Slim tried to pull off, but was side swiped. Symone hit her head on the passenger side headrest. Slim's door opened. Before he could pull his gun out, he was shot in the chest and pulled out of the Hummer and shot one more time as he laid on the ground. Masi opened his door and started shooting back. He ran to the back of the Hummer and opened Symone's door, getting her out. When she looked, she saw Muscle was shot leaning over in the backseat.

"Symone, down."

Masi jumped up and started shooting at the car of the assailants. Symone ran around the side of the Hummer and shot one of the guys two times, dropping him.

"Die, motherfucker, die."

"Symone, get back over here, it's too many of them," yelled Masi.

When Symone was about running back to the other side of the Hummer with Masi, she was shot in the back of her shoulder. She let out a scream. Before Masi could run over there to her, she was shot one more time, but the bullet grazed her head. She hit the ground hard. Her head hit the pavement, knocking her out cold. Masi was on the other side of the Hummer, still shooting at them.

"She's dead, she's dead. Come on, come."

Masi watched as they got in the car and peeled off. He ran to the side of the Hummer and picked Symone up.

"Damn, damn, don't die on me, baby girl. Fuck!" He picked her up and ran to the side of the Hummer with her in his arms. He put her in the back seat and closed the door. Then he ran around to the driver's side of the Hummer. That's when Slim grabbed his foot. Masi looked at him and picked him up, getting him in the Hummer. He jumped in the driver's seat and took off.

"Fuck, fuck, I can't go to the hospital like this, shit. Yo, Masi—"

"Slim, just hold on. I'll get ya some help. I promise, man."

"Masi, take my phone and dial KT."

No sooner had Slim passed his phone to Masi than he blacked out.

***

"Jamila, what was that about?"

"They came to ask me for help or to rat on someone, either way. I don't know shit. But Amber, I need to call my sister. So I'll be back in a few. I need to know what is going on out there."

Amber watched as Jamila walked off.

SAYNOMORE

Chapter 26

Paul had two stress balls in his hand when Joe walked in his office.

"Tell me, what happened out there?"

"Just like he said, they came riding down the street. We got them at the red light and lit their ass up."

"What about Symone, Joe? I want to know about her."

"I saw her go down. She took three to four rounds, and the last one was in her head. I saw her when she hit the ground hard."

"So she's dead is what you are telling me?"

"Yea, she's dead."

"That's all I wanted to hear. Like I said, we will not go out like the other family."

"So, what we going to do now?"

"Take back what is ours, but first let's see what happens next. And Jamila still needs to be killed now. Just because Symone is dead don't mean this war is over."

SAYNOMORE

Chapter 27

Three Days Later—

Masi was sitting in the living room, replaying how they were caught slipping. Then he heard a cough. He got up and walked in the room. He noticed Symone had her eyes opened.

"What's up, little mama? How you feeling?"

"Like I'm dead. I feel like shit. What happened?"

"We got caught slipping. They got us down bad. Slim got shot two times in the chest. Muscle got shot in the chest, the bullet went through Slim and hit Muscle, then you got shot up. They must have thought they killed you. I remember hearing someone say, *she's dead, she's dead*, then they pulled off. I thought Slim was dead too, but he grabbed my foot right before he passed out. He told me to dial KT in his phone, but I called Doctor Troy instead. When Doctor Troy picked up, I told him what happened. He told me where to go, and here we are three days later."

"Who knows what happened?" asked Symone.

"Everyone, but I ain't tell no one where you are, not even Slim or Muscle because I don't know who to trust. I do know that was a set-up. It was too perfect."

"Masi, this is what I need you to do. I need you to go see Jamila. Let her know what's going on. I haven't spoke to her in over a week. I don't need her tripping out in there."

"Symone, your phone is going off."

"Can you pass it to me please? Hello—"

"Symone, it's Lorenzo, where you at?"

"In Queens where you was at after your run-in with Detective Boatman."

"Okay, I'll be there in one hour," replied Lorenzo.

"Okay, I'll be here when you get here."

Symone hung up.

Masi, I need you to go see Jamila now."

"Okay, I'm about to go. Look, the doctor said he will be back within two to three hours. Muscle and Slim are in the room down the hall on the left. And take this—it's a brand new 9mm fully loaded. I got some clothes over there in the bag for you. It's a pair of sweatpants and a sweatshirt. I wanted to give you something that would fit and be comfortable on you."

"Thanks for everything!" said Symone.

"You know I got you, Symone."

When Lorenzo pulled up to the house, he ain't see nobody around. He got out the car, gun in hand as he walked in the house. Symone was sitting in the chair by the window. Lorenzo walked over to her and gave her a hug.

"How you feeling? Are you okay?"

"I'm a little banged up, but I'll be just fine."

"Symone, what happened?"

"Lorenzo, it all happened so fast. We was riding down a back road and the next thing I know we was getting shot at."

"Who all knew about this road?" asked Lorenzo.

"Just me, Slim, Muscle and Masi."

"That's all?"

"No but also KT, I forgot about him."

"Who was with you?"

"Masi, Slim and Muscle."

"Did KT know you was taking that road?"

"Yea, he did, we just left him."

"Symone, KT is the one who set you up to get killed. Your sister went through this with two of our childhood friends, and she killed them both. Your sister stands on loyalty. So, I see you got some new businesses. I saw the deed to the casino and the strip club."

"How you see that, Lorenzo?"

"Mr. Williams' law firm is owned by Jamila through a private friend. Only four people knew that—me, you, Jamila, her friend—and I see you gave him two hundred and ninety thousand dollars. Symone, you move just like Jamila. The only difference is that Jamila came up with nothing, and you had everything handed down to you."

"I know, Lorenzo. Where have you been for the last seven months?"

"Jamila wants me out the picture till she comes home, and I will not cross her out. I'm doing what I'm told. Well, Symone, you are doing a great job. Symone, Watch KT and stay low. You are the Princess of the city, and *Jelani's* is your kingdom now."

"So where you going now?" asked Symone.

"Back out of town. Symone, here is a number if you need me."

"Lorenzo gave Symone a kiss on the forehead before walking off.

"Lorenzo."

"Yea."

"I love you, big bro!"

"I love you more, Symone!"

Symone had a tear in her eye as she watched Lorenzo leave, and she thought about the talk they had earlier in the year. *Lorenzo told me back then Jamila might not always be around*, thought Symone. *Look now, I'm on my own.*

***

"Jamila LaCross, you have a visit."

"Here I come now."

Jamila walked to the visitation floor to see Masi sitting there waiting on her. She walked up to him and gave him a hug.

"How you doing, Jamila?"

"I'm good. I'm just trying to see what's going on out there. Where is Symone at?"

"Jamila, Symone been shot three times—leg, back and shoulder—and a bullet grazed her head."

"Who shot my little sister?" asked Jamila.

"Paul's men."

Jamila looked at Masi with a cold grill.

"Masi, tell me everything that happened."

"After you got locked up, Paul sent his men to tell Symone he wants five percent from all ya businesses. She called him up. He was very disrespectful to her, calling her the N-word, and he called you a monkey in a cage. So she killed both of them. Symone said she wasn't going for nothing at all. So he sent a team at us. They shot first and we fired back. Me, Symone, Muscle, KT and Masi paid Joe a late night visit and killed two of his men, making him sign over the casino and strip club he owned."

"How did she do that?" asked Jamila.

"She made me and Muscle hang him upside down from the 26th floor of his penthouse until he agreed to do it. She also took three hundred thousand dollars out his safe and gave the party girl he was with ten thousand dollars, and the other two hundred and ninety thousand dollars to Mr. Williams to make sure the deeds and everything else was good. She told him it was a gift from the LaCross family. Jamila, she trying to make you proud of her."

"I know, Masi—and I am. So what are her plans now?"

"I don't know. Slim got shot bad, and so was Muscle. They are out right now. We lost three men at the hotel shooting."

"Masi, I need to speak to her ASAP, right now."

"Look, when I came in, baby girl was on my dick and I walked around the metal detector. I have my phone on me if you think you can get it to the back with you."

Jamila looked around. "Yes, pass it to me under the table."

Masi passed Jamila the phone. Jamila placed the phone between her panties and waist.

"Masi, let me try to get this phone to the back."

"Okay, I'll call you in about two hours, Jamila."

"Okay, that will work," said Jamila

Masi watched as she walked back.

Jamila walked in her cell. Before she could sit down, she felt the phone vibrating. When she pulled it out, it was Symone.

"Hello, who is this and where is Masi at?"

"Symone, it's me your sister Jamila."

"How did you get Masi's phone?"

"He brung it in and passed it to me. Symone, he told me what happened, everything, but listen to me. The police came to see me yesterday about you. They are watching you, so stay low. They might be building a case against you right now. What about Paul? I know Paul. He probably thinks you are dead right now and he might try to get someone in the family to turn against you, so watch who you keep around you. Because, if he can, he will kill you. He has police working for him too, so stay out the streets. By the way, how is business doing?"

"Good. Our numbers are still up, and your friends from the Temple came to see about you last week. They said the ocean front property is under reconstruction."

"Good, I'll let you go. Just remember what I said, Symone."

"Okay, I will. I love you, big sis!"

"I love you more, beautiful."

"Jamila, hold on."

"Yea, what's up?"

"If you was home, how would you do it?" asked Symone.

"Call a meeting and have him come there. One thing I know, Symone, you can't kill a fox if it doesn't come out its fox hole."

"Thank you, sis!"

"You're welcome—and Symone, I'm proud of you."

Amber walked into the cell and saw Jamila hang up the phone.

"Hey, you going to yard?"

"Yea, I just have to put this up somewhere first."

"I got a spot you could hide it at."

Amber put Jamila's phone up before they went to yard.

"So how was your visit?" asked Amber.

"It was good. I just got an update on everything, that's all."

'So let me guess—you are about to start running?"

"No, not today, Amber, maybe tomorrow," said Jamila.

"So, what's your plans when you get out?"

"I think I'll go to Paris for a month to relax from this prison time. What about you, Amber?"

"I don't know—wherever the wind takes me, I'm going to go. So, Jamila, you have a man waiting on you out there?"

"No, I haven't had a man in over four years."

"Jamila, are you gay?"

"Hell no! I'm not."

"My bad I had to ask."

"I had a man who I truly loved, but he betrayed me three times. So I killed him and said to myself, *fuck love*. You know I never talk to no one about what I do, not even my little sister. You are the first. I guess you are starting to rub off on me."

"Well, don't ever get mad and kill me," said Amber.

"Well, don't ever make me that mad, Amber. I stand on loyalty. Always remember that. Now come on, we been walking the yard for two hours now. It's time to go in. Everyone else is going in now. Amber, watch out!"

When she turned around, she was hit in the head with a lock in a sock. Jamila tried to swing on the girl, but was hit from the back with a metal pipe that sent her dropping to her knees. Then she got hit in the stomach, making her roll over. The girl was about to hit Jamila in the face with the pipe, but she blocked it with her arm. Amber got hit two more times with the lock in the sock in the head, and she was stabbed two times. Amber was knocked out cold on the ground, with blood coming from the back of her head. They beat Jamila over and over again with the pipe and lock. They stabbed her six times. She was lying on the ground until the CO's came running outside to break it up. The alarm was going off, and pepper balls were shot at the inmates. Jamila and Amber were taken to the hospital by helicopter. Jamila had a broken arm in two places and a concussion, in addition to multiple stab wounds. Amber had two broken ribs and a concussion. They stayed in the hospital for three months. Symone ain't know nothing. She was so caught up in the war between the Scott family and hers, she ain't realize Jamila ain't been calling her. Prison authorities tried to talk with Jamila, but she ain't say a word. Amber kept quiet too. Jamila was on two types of medication, so she slept most of the time. When she opened her eyes, she saw the Captain standing next to her.

"Captain, what's up?"

"How you feel, Jamila?"

"Like hell."

"Jamila, what happened out there?"

"I don't know. It happened so fast I ain't see nobody's face."

"Well, the word is: it was the *Northside Misses*."

"Are you dead ass?" replied Jamila.

"Yea, someone paid them sixty thousand dollars to kill you," stated the captain.

"Do they think I'm dead?"

"No, but you can't go back to that side of the jail."

"Captain, I need you to work a magic trick for me. I need to go back to that same cell block and that same cell with Amber."

"Jamila, I'll see what I can do."

"I need you to pull a rabbit out the hat for me, Captain, and one more thing—I need to see Amber."

"I took care of that already. She will be moved in here with you in the next hour or so."

SAYNOMORE

Chapter 28

Slim looked at Symone. "It's been three months since they tried to kill us. You are not the same person no more."

"Slim, I was dead. No, Slim, *we* all was dead if it wasn't for Masi. So yes, I have changed. You know what? Call a meeting. I want everyone here within the next two hours, Slim. I want everyone here."

"I'll go take care of that now."

Symone walked to Jamila's bird cage. She fell in love with one of the birds. It was red with yellow, blue, and purple wings. Its back was orange, red, and green. It had long red feathers on top of its head; she named it Passion. She walked back to the glass table and lit a *black-n-mild*, waiting on everyone to come to the meeting. It was 2p.m. when everyone showed up.

"I counted thirty-eight people here, why is that?" asked Symone. There was silence, then she continued. "It's because seven of them are dead in black bags. Three months ago—myself, Slim, Muscle, and Masi would have made the body count eleven if that ugly ass fat pig had his way, but what's so funny is—that was the first time I have taken that road and to have his men waiting on us that day we took that route. So this is what I came up with. Either I was being followed or someone made a new friend that I don't know about. Let me say this—I'll find out if someone betrayed this family. If someone amongst us did, I promise you your death will not be fast. You will wish for death, rest assured. For the shit I got planned, hell has a special place just for me for the shit I be thinking about. My sister showed so much love to this family, so to spit in her face and go behind her back and try to bring this family down is so fucked up. Do you think Paul gives a fuck about a nigga, cracker or a wetback? That's what the fuck they call us behind our backs. Yea, money green and it don't have a face, but when it's gone, it's gone. But loyalty last forever, a fucking life time. There should be no haters in this family. We all have blood on our hands. The LaCross family runs seventy percent of New York City. When I say we have blood in the streets, that's what the fuck I mean. We have over fourteen dead members of the family from the beginning when Jamila started this empire ten years ago. Trust and loyalty is our foundation. I have nothing else to say."

"Symone, why don't you just put a block of C4 in his night club and kill them all?"

"Because, Masi, too many innocent lives will be killed. One block of C4 can hit the gas lines and go two to four blocks. We are talking about over a thousand lives when we just want one and who-ever stands with him."

Symone's phone went off.

"If ya don't mind, will ya excuse me while I take this call."

Symone walked out to the deck. "Hello"

"May I speak to Symone?"

"Who is this calling?"

"Deoblow."

Symone looked at her phone. "Wait, did I hear that right?"

"Yes you did."

"How did you get my number?" asked Symone.

"I have many friends like you have many friends."

"Mr. Deoblow, what can I do for you?"

"I would like to have a meeting with you if I can."

"How about Friday? And Mr. Deoblow, where would you like to have this meeting?"

"I'll call you when I get up there and we can take it from there. I'll be in touch."

When Symone walked back in, all eyes were on her.

"I said what I needed to say. Meeting over."

"Symone, let me talk to you for a second."

"You know who just called me, Slim?"

"No, who was that?"

"Mr. Deoblow."

"What you mean Deoblow?"

"Yes, Slim. Felipe's brother. He wants to have a meeting with me Friday."

"Symone, it could be a set-up."

"I know, Slim, I told him to call me when he gets up here."

"You sure that's a good idea?" replied Slim.

"I'm not sure, but I want to hear what he has to say."

"What you think Jamila going to have to say concerning your meeting with the man who put a million dollars and a hundred kilos on her head?"

"I'm just going to do what she did to his brother, get close to him, then kill him."

"So, where the meeting going to be at?"

"I don't know yet, but Slim, I got a lot to think about so can you just give me a minute to think," said Symone, frustrated.

"Sure. I got you, Symone."

Symone walked to the window. She needed to end this war. Paul had her down bad again, but his guys fucked up again. She knew she needed to kill him. She was mad because when she had her chance, she let him live and when he had his chance, he tried to kill her. She knew she wasn't Jamila, but they were going to fear her just as much. She needed to get close to him. She tortured one of his guys for days, and he wouldn't tell her where he lived. He died with honor. He was loyal all the way until the end. She walked back to her desk, took a seat, and thought about how she needed her sister for the first time. She lit a *black-n-mild* and read the sign Jamila had on her desk that said: *Tomorrow is not Promised.*

SAYNOMORE

Chapter 29

Jamila watched as they brought Amber in the room. She waited till the officer left before talking.

"Amber, are you okay?"

"Yea, I'm fine. I'm not dead and that's all that matters."

"I found out who did that to us," said Jamila.

"Who was it, Jamila?"

"It was the *Northside Misses*, what you think about that?"

"I don't remember seeing them out on yard and if they did do it, Kim is the head, they follow behind her."

"So that's who I'm going to kill."

"What about the rest of them?"

"Don't worry, Amber, I'll take care of them too."

"Amber, have you ever killed anyone?"

"No."

"Then get ready to break the ice. Do you remember how many girls jumped us?"

"It was three of them. One had a lock in the sock, and the other one had a pipe. Then you had Kim, she was the one with the knife."

"Okay, we are going to kill Kim and make the other ones wish they was dead. We are going to kill them without even touching them."

"And how are we going to do that?"

"Hit them where it's going to hurt the most, their family. Now come give me a hug."

Amber hugged Jamila.

"Amber, I promise this will never happen again."

***

"Hey, Kim, let me hit that Newport."

"Here you go. So I just got word that Jamila is coming back to the cell block."

"Who told you that, Buck?" asked Kim.

"Jason, he pulled me to the side to let me know."

"Okay, we just got to make sure the bitch dies next time."

"That's not all, Kim, the bitch knows it was us."

"So fucking what! We are the *Northside Misses*. When bitches fuck with us, they end up dead. So she coming back to this cell block?"

"I don't know. He ain't tell me all that, but she knows about the sixty thousand dollars."

"Buck, how the fuck she knows that?"

"You know these walls talk."

"Fuck it. It is what it is. Come do my shower detail."

***

"Jamila, Amber, pack it up, you're going back to the jail."

"Where at?" Jamila asked.

"Same cell block, same cell."

Jamila walked back on the cell block. All eyes were on her and Amber. Jamila and Amber caught eye contact for a minute. Everyone knew what the beef was about once they walked in the cell. There were two knifes in their locker box with a note that said: *Kim, Buck and Lady G.* During lockdown, Kim stuck her middle finger up at Jamila as she got up off the table. Jamila blew her a kiss that meant death.

"Jamila, how you want to get her?" asked Amber.

"Tomorrow morning early before breakfast."

"Where at? The bathroom?"

"No, on the stairs. There no cameras there. Amber, they are going to think we are together, so all I need you to do is stay in the doorway of the cell. If Kim see you here, she going to think I'm in the cell, but I'm not going to be. I'll be in the hallway waiting on her."

122

Chapter 30

By 4:30 a.m. the next day, Amber was in the doorway. Kim, Lady G and Buck were watching her. Kim looked at her with a smile on her face.

"Kim, you want me to handle her?"

"No, Buck, it's too many eyes—plus we got paid to kill Jamila. After we blow Jamila top, we will rock her top off."

"Kim, I ain't see Jamila yet."

"She in there, Buck, that's why Amber is in the doorway watching us. I'll be back."

"Where you going, Kim?"

"Downstairs to buy some smokes."

"You want us to come with you?"

"No, them bitches ain't going to try nothing. Just watch them and see who they talking to, and let me know what they do."

"I got you."

Amber just watched them and leaned against the door. She lit up a smoke and kept watching Buck and Lady G. Kim walked downstairs to the store lady.

"Hey, what's up, Kim?"

"Shit, I came to buy some smokes from you."

"How many you want?"

"Just four."

"You know that girl Jamila is after you."

"I ain't worried about her," said Kim.

"I know. Just be safe. There is a beat going around saying you will be dead by the end of the week"

Kim let out a laugh. "And who did you beat on?"

"You know I don't get involved in stuff like that."

"I'll catch up with you later, mama Rose."

"Okay, Kim, be safe."

Kim walked out of Mama Rose cell and was walking up the steps. She stopped on the stairs to light her Newport. She struck a match and lowered her head to light her Newport. Just then, Jamila came from behind, grabbed her by the neck and rammed her knife in her stomach. Kim took a deep breath. Jamila turned the knife sideways and said in her ear: "I do this shit for real, bitch. The look on your face got my pussy wet. Don't worry, Lady G and Buck is next." Jamila jammed the knife two more times in her stomach, and one time in her side, dropping her down to her knees. Kim looked up at Jamila. Jamila jammed the knife in her neck and ripped it out. Jamila pushed her body down the stairs. Mama Rose saw everything. Jamila looked at her and put her finger to her lips, then winked at Mama Rose as she walked back up the stairs. She wiped off the knife with a rag and dropped it off the side of the stairs. Lady G and Buck looked at Jamila as she walked past them with a smile on her face. They jumped off the table and ran to the stairs to see Kim lying dead in a pool of blood, looking up in space with her eyes open. All they heard was an alarm going off and CO's yelling. "Lock it down, lock it down!" It was 5:30 that morning when Kim got killed, and the prison was on lock down.

Chapter 31

"Masi, what's rocking?"

"Shit, just making my rounds. What's good with you, bro?"

"Shit, I'm just macking. I thought KT made the pick up?"

"Shit, Symone changed a lot of shit around, Muscle. She called me this morning and told me to make the pick-ups"

"Shit, it's her world. Now let me go get that for you."

"Hold up just a minute. I got you, Muscle."

Masi looked around the hotel at how Symone had everyone lined up. She really changed a lot of shit around.

"Yo, Masi, here you go, my guy."

"How much is this?"

"Twenty-seven thousand dollars on the head."

"Cool, let me go finish these rounds up."

"Say less. Peace, my nigga."

"A'ight, bro. Stay safe, Muscle."

***

Symone was watching the news when her phone went off.

"Hello?"

"Symone, what's the word for today?"

"Slim, I have the meeting with Diablo at five-thirty p.m. today. I want you, Muscle and Masi with me."

"What about KT?" asked Slim.

"I want him out the picture for a little while. I ain't vibing with him right now. Something ain't right with him, I can feel it."

"You still thinking about that hit?"

"Slim, how can I forget it? You got hit up. Muscle got hit up. I got hit up too. We was over with if it wasn't for Masi thinking fast. Slim, shit got real fast when I got shot. I just knew I was dead."

"When the last time you talked to Jamila?"

"It's been a while, but after the meeting I'll go see her. Look, it's twelve p.m. right now. I got three hours before the meeting. You go make sure everyone is ready and we are having the meeting at *Destiny's.*"

"Okay, I'll get on that now."

Symone had barely put her phone down when it started to beep. She looked and saw she had a call coming in from a blocked number.

"Hello. Symone speaking"

"Hello, Symone, I have some information for you."

"Who am I speaking to?" asked Symone.

"That's not important."

"If you not going to tell me your name, how I know this information is right? Because I can always use information."

"I'll let you be the judge of that," the anonymous caller said, then Symone's phone went dead within three seconds. Symone got six pictures of KT with Paul together, showing KT getting in Paul's limo at the casino. Three more photos showed KT at Paul's diner taking money from him. Then Symone got a text that said, *He got paid $150,000 to set you up and to tell him all the places you be at.*

Symone looked at the pictures one more time, then put her phone down and went to get ready for her meeting.

***

It was 2:43 p.m. when Symone walked into *Destiny's.* She walked past Slim, Muscle, and Masi, then went right to the ballroom and sat down at the back table. When they walked in, Symone looked at them.

"Tomorrow, I want a meeting with everyone at the waste plant at seven p.m. Masi and Muscle, I need you two to take care of something for me tonight."

Slim shook his head, confused. It was 3 p.m. when Mr. Deoblow and three of his men walked into the ballroom, accompanied by two of Symone's men. Symone got up and shook his hand, and his men's hands as well.

"Mr. Deoblow, nice to meet you."

"Likewise, Symone."

"Can I get you or your men something to drink?"

"Yes, please."

"Masi, can you please bring me a bottle of Vodka over here with five glasses?"

"Symone, I believe me and your sister got off on the wrong foot, so I'm hoping we can start off better. Symone, I been locked up for five years. Two years ago, your sister killed my brother."

"I am very much aware of that, just like I know you are aware that twenty-seven years ago your brother killed our father in the worst way," replied Symone.

"I am. We both have blood spilled on both sides. I see the way you run your family. You play for keeps. I respect that, Symone."

At that point, Masi walked back to the table with the drinks."

"Thanks, Masi!"

Everyone took a shot.

"Mr. Deoblow, you put one million dollars on my sister's head. So are you here to let me know you are pulling the contract off her?"

"Yes, I'm here to pay my respects."

Mr. Deoblow snapped his fingers, and one of his men handed Slim a suitcase with $1 million in it.

"The contract is off. I would like to do business with the La-Cross family"

"All business goes through my sister first," replied Symone. "Anyway, what type of business is it?"

"I have the purest cocaine money can buy, and I will give you as much as you need for the lowest price."

"Mr. Deoblow, I will talk to my sister and let her know everything you said today."

"Thank you, Symone!"

"Do you have a direct number I can call you on, Mr. Deoblow?"

"Yes, I do." Mr. Deoblow handed Symone his card.

"Thank you. I will be in touch."

Mr. Deoblow got up with his men and walked out.

"Symone, what do you think of that?"

"I don't know, Slim, I don't trust him. I have a feeling it's more to him. I have to go see Jamila. Masi count the money, put it in a paper bag and throw the suitcase away. I'm going out the back door to go see Jamila. Slim, have everyone ready for the meeting."

Symone rode around Queens for an hour, then through Brooklyn until she made it to the jail. She walked to the attorney's room and was waiting on Jamila. Ten minutes later, Jamila walked in the room.

"How you been?" Jamila said as she walked up and gave Symone a hug.

"I been good, big sis."

"And how is the family?"

"Good, everything is everything."

"Symone, what is that smell coming off of you? I know that scent."

"Mr. Deoblow's scent must have rubbed off of me."

"Did I hear you right, Symone?" asked Jamila.

"Yes, that's what I came to talk to you about."

"Symone, you had a meeting with the man who tried to kill me?"

"I know he put money on your head, but I ain't know he tried to kill you."

Jamila got up and showed Symone her back and arms.

"Yea, three months ago he paid some girls in here sixty thousand dollars to kill me."

Symone put her hands over her mouth. "Sis, I ain't know that happened. Why you ain't call me?"

"I was in the hospital. I just got back a few days ago."

"Who in here did that to you? I will kill their whole fucking family." Symone sounded upset.

"I killed one of them already."

"So you are the one they was talking about here when I came in."

"What was this meeting about with Deoblow?" Jamila asked.

"He took the contract off of you and gave the family the $1 million, and he wants to do business with our family."

"No business at all," said Jamila. "See where his loyalty is at. Have him kill Paul. Those are the rules. When the contract is pulled off, the hitman becomes the mark. So, have him kill Paul and give him a deadline."

"Okay. I will, Jamila, but I also want you to look at these. This is KT taking money from Paul. Yea, I got them this morning."

"How did you get these?"

"I got a phone call this morning asking me if I wanted some information. I said yes, and these pictures come through with this text."

"Symone, before Morwell was killed, he taught me two different kinds of respect. You have a lot of the members' respect, but you have to make them fear you. Kill his mother, sister and child in the worst way."

"I'll do it tomorrow night at the waste plant."

"Symone, this is Captain Wade's address. She helped me kill that bitch who did this to me. Give her a diamond chain and a hundred thousand dollars and if she takes it, make her a part of the family. Also have her at the meeting too."

"I will. I love you, Jamila."

"I love you more, Symone!"

Symone gave Jamila a kiss on the cheek and left to do what her sister told her to do. Jamila walked back to her cell. Every officer was looking at her. She knew what they were looking at as she smiled to herself.

***

It was 9:30 p.m. when Symone had the black Hummer limo pulled up at Captain Wade's house. Slim got out, then went and knocked on Captain Wade's door. When she opened the door, she looked at Slim.

"Can I help you?"

"Someone would like to talk to you, Captain Wade."

She turned her head, looking at her son and sister asleep on the couch and said, "Okay."

Her sister got up. "Kia, where are you going?"

Slim looked at her. "Nowhere, she will be right back."

"I'll be right back, sis."

She looked at Slim one more time before walking to the limo. Once she got there, Masi opened the door for her to get in. Masi stayed outside the limo as Captain Wade and Symone talked. When she got in the limo, Symone was smoking a *black-n-mild*. She looked at Tasha.

"How are you doing, Tasha?"

"I'm good."

"Do you know who I am?"

"No, I don't."

"My name is Symone LaCross."

"Okay, you are Jamila's sister."

"Yes, I'm her younger sister."

"How can I help you?"

"My sister wanted to thank you for what you did for her."

Symone handed her the bag with the $100,000 in it. Tasha was surprised when she saw all the money in the bag.

"Is this for me?"

"Yes, it is. It's hundred thousand dollars in that bag. Tasha, my sister runs seventy percent of New York City. We play for keeps. You helped her, so she is giving you a chance to be a part of this family. If you say yes, there is no turning back. If you say no, the respect will still be there because you helped her. So what do you say, Tasha?"

Tasha looked at Symone and closed her eyes; when she opened them, she said, "Yes."

Symone smiled. "I'm glad you said yes. I have something for you.

Symone gave her two guns—a Glock 9 and a .380—then she handed her a black diamond chain.

"Tasha, never take this chain off. If you do so, it's a sign of disrespect. Tasha, I'm coming to get you tomorrow night around eight-thirty p.m., so be ready. Wear all black and gray. We don't dress like thugs or ho's. Here's ten thousand dollars for your clothes. Always keep your guns on you, and remember I'll be here tomorrow night for you. You are a part of this family now, Tasha LaCross."

Symone gave her a hug, and tapped on the window two times, then Masi opened the door. He saw Tasha with everything, and gave her a hug.

"Tasha, welcome to the family."

Tasha walked past Slim, smiling. She walked in her house and looked at the limo as it drove off.

"What was that all about, sis, and who was that?"

"I can't tell you who that was, but I can tell you I'm a part of the LaCross family now."

"For real? I knew it was something big, I could tell."

Tasha went upstairs with her bags.

SAYNOMORE

Chapter 32

It was 6:30 that morning. The jail was still on lockdown. The food cart was going door to door, when Captain Wade opened Jamila's door. Jamila looked at her neck, and they both smiled at each other.

"What time that happen, Captain?" asked Jamila.

"Around nine-thirty last night. I have a meeting to go to tonight at eight-thirty."

"I know already."

Captain Wade looked at her, winked at her and closed the door, walking off to the next door to feed. Jamila sat on the bed, knowing that Tasha was the first person she put down in over seven years, but she saw her loyalty in her.

***

Symone sat back, smoking her *black-n-mild*. She pulled out her phone and called Mr. Deoblow. He picked up after two rings.

"Hello, Symone."

"Mr. Deoblow, I'll make this quick. I talked to her and she said, *prove your loyalty*. When you pulled the contract off of her, it goes on the one who agreed to the contract. So she said."

"She is right and I will be in touch, Symone."

Deoblow hung up the phone and took a sip of his wine. Symone took a pull of her *black-n-mild*. It was 7:45 p.m. when she put the *black-n-mild* in the ashtray and walked outside her front door where Slim and Masi was waiting on her at.

"Is everyone at the waste plant?"

"Yea, Muscle made sure everyone is there, even the two new guys—Iceman and Pistol Pete."

"Good, now take me to pick up Tasha."

***

"Sis, you look like a mobster. Where you going?"

"I don't know. Even if I did, I couldn't tell you, sis."

"Tasha, just be safe."

"I will."

"That limo is outside for you again."

"Okay. I got to go, sis, I love you."

"I love you, big sis."

Symone watched as Tasha came out the house. Masi got out to open the door for her.

"What you think about her, Symone?"

"I like her. She look like a boss bitch. Jamila had picked her because she saw something in her, Slim." When Tasha got in the limo, she gave Symone and Slim a hug.

"Tasha, do you have your two guns on you?"

"Yes, right here, Symone."

"Good. We never want to get caught slipping, beautiful."

They made it to the waste plant. All of them got out of the limo. Tasha looked confused as they walked inside. Everyone was standing up, looking at Symone as she walked in. No one was saying a word. Muscle walked up and said something in Symone's ear, then went to his seat. Once Symone sat down, everyone took their seats.

"Everyone, meet Tasha, Iceman and Pistol Pete," said Symone. "I called everyone here tonight because I went to see Red Invee, and she has a message for everyone here, but we will talk about that later."

Symone got up and walked around the table. Once she got to KT, she walked past him, then she turned around real fast with her gun out and smacked him in the face, knocking him down to the floor. Muscle and Masi grabbed his arms. She then smacked him in the face one more time with the gun as they held his arms. She took both his guns he had on him, and placed them on the table. KT had blood coming from his head. Everyone was looking at Symone.

"This piece of shit gave his loyalty up for one hundred and fifty thousand dollars, but I'll show everyone here I ain't no ho'. You ain't going to try me at all. Tie his fucking ass up to that table now."

Symone looked at Slim Boogie and nodded. He got up from the table and walked off. He came back a few seconds later with three people with bags over their heads, and their hands tied behind their backs.

"Slim, hook them up to those chains."

Symone walked up to them and pulled them bags off their heads.

"KT, open your fucking eyes. See who is here to see you. See what the fuck you did. You killed your mother, son and sister."

She looked around at everyone. "I told ya not to fuck with me, right? Did I not tell ya I will kill your whole fucking family? I don't play. If anyone of ya talk about what ya see tonight or betray this family, this will be you up here. Masi, show them the pictures."

Masi showed them the pictures of KT getting money from Paul.

"I got shot three times. Slim got shot twice in the chest. Muscle got shot one time in the chest. Three of us would have been dead if it wasn't for Masi that day four months ago. KT, I made you a made man."

She walked up to the table and picked up the bat. She looked at everyone and smacked KT in the face with the bat. The air was filled with screams coming from his mother, sister, and son. KT was dizzy from the blow to his face from the bat. Tasha couldn't believe what she was seeing.

With a very weak voice, KT looked up at Symone. "Symone, please don't do this, please don't."

"Fuck you, pussy."

Symone looked at Crystal. "Come here, Crystal."

Crystal got up and walked to Symone.

"What you think about him?"

"He's a piece of shit and a disloyal motherfucker."

"I'm glad you said that."

Symone handed Crystal the bat. "Break his legs."

Crystal took the bat and was smacking his legs until everyone heard the bones breaking. KT was screaming in agony. Symone walked up to him. "Do that hurt, boo? Not the big bad KT anymore, huh?" With all the blood pouring from his mouth, and the tears in his eyes, as a result of the pain, he couldn't talk.

"Crystal, go sit back down."

Symone took the bat from her.

"Slim, how do your chest feel?"

"I can still feel the bullets breaking up in my fucking chest."

"Slim, I want five teeth out of his mouth."

Symone handed him the baseball bat. Slim looked at KT and smacked him in the face with the bat, breaking his jaw and knocking three teeth out his mouth. KT was shaking in excruciating pain.

"Slim, I said five teeth, not three."

Slim looked at Symone again, and hit KT two more times, taking three more teeth out his mouth. There was blood everywhere. KT was unconscious.

"Muscle, you was in the car, wasn't you?" asked Symone.

"Yea."

"How do you feel?"

"Fucked up."

Symone handed him the bat. Muscle beat KT in the chest over and over till he broke his ribs and had them poking through his skin. His body went into shock from all the pain. His mother passed out, and his sister was crying out loud. Symone looked at KT's half dead body and at everyone else.

"Tasha, come up here."

Once Tasha got up there, Symone looked at her.

"So, Tasha, what do you think of them all?" asked Symone.

"If they are a part of his blood line, fuck them, true facts."

"I'm glad you said that. Go get one of his guns off the table and come back up here with it."

When Tasha walked back up there, Symone looked at her. "Shoot him in the head."

Tasha looked at KT. "The LaCross family stands on loyalty," she said, then shot KT in the head two times. His body went limp. She then pointed the gun at his sister. Symone nodded, and Tasha pulled the trigger. Blood went everywhere, blowing his sister's head off. She then pointed the gun at his mother.

"No, Tasha, give me the gun and go back to your seat."

Symone looked at KT's dead body, then his sister's dead body hanging on the chains. She looked at everyone, pointed the gun at his mother and shot her six times in the chest. Then she walked up to his seven-year-old son. She closed her eyes and thought about what Jamila told her. *"You have to make them fear you. They respect you, but they have to fear you."* She opened her eyes, put the gun to his head and looked at everyone. Then she pulled the trigger, blowing his brains out. His body jumped back and went limp. She walked up and placed the gun next to KT's dead body. Afterwards, she walked to the table and sat down, looking at everyone.

"Please don't call my fucking bluff. The Queen is working on her case, trying to come home soon. She's proud of all of you. The LaCross family will not fall under my watch. I really hope I have all of your loyalty now. Do I have your loyalty now?"

Everyone said *yes* at the same time.

"Slim, Muscle and Masi, get three people and take care of this mess. Everyone else, be at *Jelani's* Monday by three p.m." Crystal, Tasha and Symone walked to Jamila's office. Masi and everyone else Symone told to clean up swung into the task. They burned the bodies and table, pouring acid on the floor to clean up the blood.

"Crystal, you been a part of this family way before me. Tasha, my sister took a liking to you. There are only three females in this family—three of us and my sister the Queen. So we have to show these guys that we are just as strong as they are, and we are not scared to take a life. That's why I called you two up there with me."

Masi walked in the office. "It's done, Symone."

"Good. Can you take Crystal and Tasha home for me, please?"

"Sure."

Symone looked at them as they walked out the office. It was 1 a.m. When Tasha made it home, she went to the room to see her sister and son asleep, then she went and took a shower. She never killed nobody before. Nevertheless, she did what she needed to do to make sure it wasn't her sister nor son on the chains, or her on that table she'd seen tonight. That's when she realized, *"You fuck up, you die!"*

SAYNOMORE

Chapter 33

The jail was off lockdown, and the inmates were back active. Tasha walked up to Jamila as she was standing next to the yard gate.

"Symone don't play no games."

"I know, Captain. She can be heartless, but sometimes you have to strike fear into the hearts of the people around you. I see they moved Lady G and Buck."

"Yea, they went to P.C. Jamila, you was under the gun. Everyone know you did it, but no one would come forward and tell on you, and the cameras ain't see nothing."

"Tasha, no witness, no weapons, no proof, no crime," said Jamila.

Tasha smiled when Jamila said that. The alarm went off, letting them know that yard call was over. Jamila walked back in her cell and sat down on the bed, looking at Amber.

"Amber, we both have three years left, and I was thinking I want you to be a part of my family."

"For real, Jamila?"

"For real, Amber, what you say?" asked Jamila.

Amber got up and gave Jamila a hug.

"So what's my name now, Amber LaCross?"

"Amber LaCross—hmm—I like it. It has a nice ring to it."

***

It's been four days since Symone killed KT and his family. She was lying on the bed. KT was her homie, but she remembered what Jamila told her about how she killed two of her childhood friends for disloyalty. So she knew she had to do it no matter what. Within the last two years she killed over fifteen people, got shot three times, got a casino and a strip club. She looked at the man dead in the face who tried to kill her sister, and shook his hand. One thing she couldn't stop thinking about was the sign that was on Jamila's desk that said, "*Tomorrow's not Promised.*" She lost her thoughts when her phone went off.

"Hello."

"What's up, Symone? It sounds like you are still in bed."

"I am. What's up, Slim?"

"I was calling to see what the meeting is about tomorrow."

"I'm giving everyone a gift. Besides, I have a big meal for everyone and I'ma talk about when Jamila comes home." Symone

"Fact, what time is all this taking place?"

"Two-thirty p.m.—and Slim, I think I'll go see my mother and sister today. Did Muscle make the pick up today?"

"Yea, he did."

"Okay, have him run *Destiny's* for now and I'll try and catch up with you later tonight at *Passions*. If not, I'll see you tomorrow at the meeting."

"Okay. Just call me, Symone," said Slim.

"I will."

Symone hung up the phone, closed her eyes, and went back to her thoughts.

***

Tasha was looking in the mirror at her black diamond chain in the bathroom. She knew there wasn't no turning back. Last night was her first time killing someone. She had no choice in the matter. *That could have been me and my family on those chains*, Tasha thought. She knew what she signed up for, but she damn sure ain't think she would have to kill no one her first night. Not only one person, but two. Jamila put her stamp on her, and four nights ago shit got real. When she walked out the bathroom, she had a new attitude and new rules to follow. One: *loyalty above all things*. Two: *trust your family*. Three: *always stay with two guns*. Four: *never take your chain off*. Five: *respect the code of silence*. She had to be at *Jelani's* tomorrow at 3 p.m. for a meeting. She'd never been there, but she knew where it was at.

Chapter 34

When Symone pulled up to her mother's house, she saw Victorious playing outside in the front yard. Jamila moved her mother and sister to Long Island a few years back. When Symone got out the car, Victorious ran up to her and gave her a hug.

"Symone, Symone!"

"Hey, beautiful, how you been?"

"Good, I miss you!"

"I miss you more!"

"Symone, what took you so long to come see me?" asked Victorious.

"I been real busy, baby, but I got something for you."

"What you got for me?"

"You have to guess first."

Victorious looked in the car. "I see, I see you got me a puppy."

"I sure did. Let me go get her out the car."

"What's her name, Symone?"

"You have to give her a name, Victorious, that's up to you."

"I'll name her Pebbles."

"Okay, where is mom at?" asked Symone.

"She is in the house cooking."

"Okay, let me go say hi. I'll be back in a few."

Symone opened the door. "Mom, you in here?"

"Who is that?"

"Oh, my godchild, where have you been? Long time no see." She hugged Symone. "You look so beautiful. Come in the kitchen and let me introduce you to my friend—Miss Little. Miss Little, this is my daughter. Symone, this is Miss Little."

"Nice to meet you, Miss Little."

"Nice to meet you too, Symone." Miss Little looked askance at Symone's godmother and said: "Why you ain't tell me your daughter was the one who did that big donation for the city of New York?"

"You know I don't talk a lot, girl."

"Mom, mom, look what Symone got me!" screamed Victorious.

"Symone, I know you ain't get that girl no dog."

"Yes, I did, mom, you said when you get a house with a yard, she can have one."

"Symone, I'll kill you."

"I'll catch up with you later," Miss Little said. "I'll let ya talk," she added.

"Okay," Symone's stepmom replied.

"Sandy, I'll see you later. Take care, Symone."

"You too, Miss Little. So how you been, mom?"

"Good, I been missing you. You don't stop by no more."

"Mom," said Symone, "I'm sorry. From Jamila going to jail and me running everything, it's a lot on me."

"I saw it on the news. She was in handcuffs. I was so hurt and upset at the same time."

"I know, mom, she will be home soon. It's only a few more years."

"That girl is just like her father, smart, fearless, and—if it ain't family—heartless. I hope you ain't out there killing people too."

"Mom, I don't have the nerve to do that. By the way, where is Victorious' dad at?"

"Me and him split up a few months ago. All he wanted to do was drink and spend money. I decided to revert to my former name of Mrs. Catwell."

"I understand. It smells good in here, what are you cooking?"

"It's Sunday, girl. I'm cooking everything. You stay for dinner?"

"Yes, I am. I was hoping I could stay the night."

"Baby, you know you will always have a bed here. Something must be on your mind. What's wrong? Baby, talk to mom."

Mrs. Catwell grabbed Symone by the hand, and walked her to the couch. Symone laid her head on her shoulders. "What's wrong with my child?"

"Mom, I just want God to forgive me on my day of judgement. Mom, I did so many things I can't take back. What you don't know is that Jamila is in jail because of my actions, not hers. She is suffering from what I did."

"That's your big sister, Symone. She knows where your heart is at, and God forgives all. Baby, if you really meant it from the heart, then believe God will forgive you. God knows what you are going to do before you do it. It's all written in the book of life. You just have to make better choices in life. I know there is blood on your hands even though you told me earlier that you don't have the nerve to kill someone. I was so mad at Jamila I stopped talking to her for years. I was afraid I was going to lose her like I did your father, but you know what? She still loved me, and I still loved her. She made sure my bills were paid every month and I wanted for nothing. She was her father all over again. And I know one day Victorious is going to follow behind you two and pull up in a sixty-thousand-dollar car just like you did today."

"I love you so much, mom."

"I love you too, child. Now come on, let's pray and eat. Can you call your sister in here? Symone, how much is that dog going to cost me?"

"Don't worry, mom, I have everything in the car."

"Symone, if that dog eats up my stuff, I'll call you and beat you when you get here. And then you are going to take me shopping."

SAYNOMORE

Chapter 35

Slim saw Muscle standing outside the hotel, and walked up to him. "What's up, bro?"

"Shit, Slim, just watching the scene. What brings you by?"

"Symone hit me up and told me to tell you—you have the hotel now."

"I knew that shit was coming. Where she at now?"

"I don't know. She got her phone cut off. I tried calling her a few times."

"Shit, Slim, she might be getting some dick."

"She needs some," said Slim.

They both started laughing.

"Slim, don't forget about Jamila. After what I saw the other night, the look in her eyes, Slim, Symone don't give no fucks."

"Facts, Muscle, KT was tripping. I don't know what got in his head. Look, I got to make some runs, so I'll pull up later."

"Hold up a second, Slim, where Lorenzo been at?" asked Muscle.

"Symone told me Jamila don't want him in the picture right now, not until she comes home. She gave the candlestick to Symone until she touch back down, but I got to pull up on Masi. So I'll catch up with you later, Muscle."

"Peace, Slim."

***

"Joe, you told me Symone was dead three months ago. I believed you, but I done seen her more than one time. Well, I don't care because she got the message."

"And what kind of message you sent, Paul?"

"Hold that thought, Joe, my phone is ringing. Hello."

"Hello, Paul, it's Deoblow. How are you doing today?"

"I'm good, Mr. Deoblow."

"So Paul, I was seeing if you can come down here for a visit?"

"I'm really busy up here with the LaCross family. Can you make a trip up here?"

"Sure I can, how do Saturday sound?" asked Deoblow.

"That sounds good to me, Mr. Deoblow, I'll see you then." Paul hung up.

"Joe, is Jamila dead yet?"

"I don't know. I know she was flown to the hospital and she was stabbed a few times."

"Find out for me, and we going to throw a party for Mr. Deoblow when he comes up here Saturday. I want him killed. He's going to have a car pull up when he gets here, and I want over five hundred rounds put in his car. I want him dead, no questions asked. Then I want his head put in a box and sent to Symone. That's the message I want her to have. We will kill him and make them think this war is over. Then we turn right around and kill them. We have to play this like it's a game of chess."

"I'm on it now, Paul."

"You know what, Joe? The Scott family done killed over and over and won five wars in New York City. We took over Chinatown and other parts of New York City. So I asked myself, how did we let a nigga come out of nowhere and take over Queens?"

"The pieces fell in the right place for her from Fabio to Frankie, and the cards was dealt in her favor. Well, I'll go get things setup for Saturday."

Mob Ties 4

Chapter 36

It was 2:15 when Symone made it to *Jelani's*. She had six bottles of Gray Goose on ice. The whole table was covered with varieties of food. When everyone got there, it was 3 o'clock on the dot. Everyone had on black and gray. The waiters were passing out drinks to everyone. Symone took her spoon and tapped her glass to get everyone's attention. All eyes were on her when she stood up.

"Love, loyalty, respect, and honor, I got a call last night from Paul Scott that said, *You won—the war is over.*"

Everyone started clapping. "This meal is for us. We lost friends to this war. We killed the ones who wasn't loyal to this family because of this war, but still we stand. My sister started this family over ten years ago. Now look where we stand. We are on top, and this is just the beginning for us. I'm asking everyone here to raise your glasses right now for the ones who ain't here who died for this family. May they sleep in peace. And for the Queen who made this possible for us, Jamila. We are toasting to the fallen family members and to the Queen Red Invee. Slim, can you please pass everyone here one of the envelopes. In these envelopes you will find $20,000 as a bonus for winning this war and for staying loyal to this family. Enjoy your meal everyone."

Tasha walked to the window and looked out of it as Symone followed her.

"What's on your mind, beautiful?"

"I heard stories about your sister, how she was just a killer until I met her. I drove past this place every day and wondered how it was in here. Now I'm a part of the LaCross family, and your sister is not the picture everyone who don't know her is painting. She takes care of her own. She just wants us to win at life."

"Tasha, just wait until Jamila comes home. Everything will be in its rightful place. My sister is funny, smart and very dangerous when it comes down to it."

"Trust me, I know already, Symone, how she can become. She plays no games at all."

"Tasha, everyone here made it because we are family. I done kill over twenty people for this family. You done killed two so far. Being in the Mafia is scary sometimes, but as long as you stay loyal, we will always stand next to you. Now come on, let's finish eating."

Symone looked around one more time at everyone, smiled to herself, and lifted up her glass to the LaCross family.

SAYNOMORE

Chapter 37

"Paul, everyone is in place. How long before Deoblow gets here?"

"He's on his way now, and I want that fucking pig dead. He thinks he could put the press on me. Do he know who the fuck I am? After today I won't have to worry about his ass no fucking more. I called Symone last night and told her she won the war. The first step to winning this war is to disarm your enemy, and that's what I did last night. Now I'll take care of Mr. Deoblow."

"So how you want it done again?"

"As soon as I walk out the door, you light that bitch the fuck up."

"Excuse me, Mr. Scott, Mr. Deoblow's car just pulled up."

"Thank you, Joe. It's show time. Let's get this shit over with."

Paul walked out the front door. He looked around and was about walking toward Mr. Deoblow's limo. As soon as he took his first step, he was shot two times in the chest with a high-powered assault rifle blowing him back two steps, killing him right there on the spot. His body was shaking with blood coming from his mouth. Joe looked up and took two steps back inside the building. The limo drove off. Everyone ran to see Paul's dead body, taking pictures of him lying there dead. Joe walked to the bar, and saw a man sitting there. He handed Joe a suitcase with $75,000 inside, then he walked away.

Right then he received a phone call. "Hello?"

"Did you receive our suitcase?"

"Yes."

"Then it's done, Joe, I will be in touch."

Joe looked at his phone, put it in his pocket and walked off.

***

Jamila was sitting in the TV room of the jail, watching the news.

"Breaking news. Paul Scott—the head of the Scott family—was gunned down today at 3 p.m. in front of his own place of business. He was shot two times in the chest, killing him. This was the first

attempt on his life that was fatal. Witnesses say he walked outside to head to a limo that was waiting on him. That's when he was assassinated. This could be connected to the recent war that's been going on for the last two and a half years in New York City. No one is taking questions at this time, but keep your channel tuned in here for more updates to come."

Jamila walked out the TV room. She went to sit down and play chess with Miss Peterson.

***

Symone was smoking her *black-n-mild,* watching the news when she saw the picture of Paul Scott on the TV screen. She smiled to herself and thought about the sign on Jamila's desk that said, *"Tomorrow is not Promised."* She knew Deoblow had it done, and the door to the new relationship she just opened. She thought about all the conversations she had with Paul, and how he always tried to get over on her. Now he's dead, looking up at the skies from a lifeless body. She put her *black-n-mild* out and said to herself: "I will not lose."

***

Joe walked in the room. All eyes were on him waiting for him to speak.

"Paul is dead and there ain't shit we can do about it. Now the question is who did it?"

"Joe, we all know the LaCross family is behind his killing. That nigga Symone had it done."

"Are you sure, Bobby?"

"Who else we been at war with, Joe?"

"You have a point. But, Bobby, I don't think it was her. Paul and Deoblow been having words lately because he took the one million dollars from him. But from this point on, we need to start working on our family and start building us back up. No more wars, just good business from here on out. I don't care how no one looks at it—Red Invee is the Queen Don. We are not throwing in the white flag, but we need to move smarter before we die. We don't know who she has working for her, but the first step of business is to get out properties back."

"And Joe, how you expect to do that?"

"I'll see if I can have a sit-down with Symone this week after Paul's funeral. We are going to end this war and make this family what it used to be."

SAYNOMORE

Chapter 38

It was ten in the morning. The FBI and NYPD were outside, taking pictures of everyone at Paul's burial. The heads of every family were talking in a circle when Symone's limo pulled up. All eyes were on her. Symone had on an all-black dress with black shoes. Her hair was pulled to the back. She walked up to the circle of bosses with Slim and Masi behind her. Muscle stayed by the limo, watching everyone.

"Hello, families."

"Symone."

"Symone LaCross, I never had the chance to meet you. I only heard stories about you. To my understanding, you are Red Invee's little sister."

"I am and may I ask who I am talking to?" asked Symone.

"My name is Mr. Gambino. I'm the head of the Gambino family. I'm asking you and Joe here together, is this war over between the two of you? Because this war is making it hard for us standing here today to do business in our burrows. We have the police cracking down on us harder than ever before."

"Mr. Gambino, I have no problem with Joe Scott. I don't understand why everyone shoots at our family, and I say this with the utmost respect. First, it started with the Lenacci family, then Deniro family, and now the Scott family. We never started with none of you. We give all of you the utmost respect. So I stand here in front of everyone when I say as far as the war goes, it is over on the LaCross side."

Everyone looked at Joe. "Symone, I'm not going to sit here and act like you ain't have me hanging upside down twenty-six stories up, but I am the new Don of the Scott family and Paul was wrong to take a hit up on the Queen Don. That's what cost us all this blood in the streets on both sides. But, I did talk to my family already about this and on my side as well, the war is over."

Joe walked up and gave Symone a hug, and a kiss on the left cheek. Symone gave him a kiss on the right cheek and just like that the war was over.

"Joe, I am sorry for your family's losses."

"Thank you. Likewise, Symone."

"Detective Green, you taking pictures of all of this?"

"Yea, I am, Agent Carter."

"So that's the Queen of the city's little sister—Symone?"

"Yea, that's her, Carter."

"What can you tell me about her, Green?"

"She is a killer, a cold-hearted one ten times worse than her sister—Jamila. I have reason to believe she is the one who killed Detective Boatman."

"What is that reason?" asked Carter.

"Detective Boatman was killed at ten-thirty p.m. and set on fire. At eleven-fifteen p.m. there is a call about a car on fire not even twenty minutes away from where Detective Boatman was killed. Guess whose car it was? If you think Symone LaCross, then you are right."

"So let me guess, Green," said Carter, "she reported the car stolen?"

"Yea, she did, and the only witness was an old lady who was gunned down. I have reports of her having Paul's nightclub shot up, killings in limos. She bullied Joe out of his casino and strip club."

"How she do that?" asked Carter.

"She hung him upside down from the twenty-sixth floor of his penthouse suite."

"Green, how do you know all of that?"

"Come on, Carter, you should know there is a snitch in everyone's family."

"So who the snitch in the LaCross family?"

"I haven't found him yet, but I'm looking for the weak link."

"So, Green, if you know all of this, why don't ya bring her in?"

"Nobody is going to get on stand against the LaCross family. Mr. Deniro, from the Deniro family, was killed on a private prison bus, but nobody knew the location or when he was going to get transported."

"Money talks and he ended up dead with three rounds to his head, and the DA who was working the case came up missing. Him and his driver three weeks later popped up dead, and D.A. Moore was missing his head."

"Look, Green, she is giving him a white rose and a red one. Why you think that is for?" asked Carter.

"The white rose is for the innocent lives, and the red one is for the blood that was spilled between families."

"You got all of these pictures?"

"Yea, two thousand of them. Come on, Carter let's get out of here."

SAYNOMORE

Chapter 39

Symone walked into *Jelani's* to find Oso sitting at the bar. He was smoking a Cuban cigar with four of his men around him. Symone talked to Oso a few times, but this was the first time she was seeing him face to face. He had on a white suit with a pink shirt and pink Stacy Adams on with no socks. He had on a gold chain and a gold watch with diamonds around the face. He was bald. She couldn't help but notice he was big boned, but not fat. She could tell he meant business. He got up and walked to her. "Hello, Symone," he said to her as he gave her a hug and kiss on the cheek.

"Hello, Oso, how was your trip up here?"

"It was long, but I'm here."

"So tell me, what was so important that we had to meet within twenty-four hours?" asked Symone curiously.

"My brother had a very strong relationship with your sister Red Invee before his death. He also had a very strong relationship with Paul Scott. Now Mr. Scott is dead. I know the LaCross family was at war with the Scott family. So here is the problem, Symone. Paul would spend close to ten thousand dollars a month with us, but now that he is dead, we need someone to fulfill his contract with us."

"Oso, please come sit down at the table with me. Masi, can you bring me a bottle of Cîroc with two glasses. Oso, if I'm right about this, your family been doing business with my family over nine years now. And yes, we was at war with the Scott family, but Paul's blood is not on my hands. I could have killed him plenty of times, but I didn't."

Oso looked as Masi brought the two glasses and bottle of Cîroc to the table. He watched as Symone poured both of them a shot.

"So whose hands are Paul's blood on?" asked Oso.

Symone took her shot, then lit her *black-n-mild* before answering Oso's question. "Deoblow killed him."

Oso took his shot, then Symone poured herself another shot.

"Why would Deoblow kill him?"

"Because the contract he put on Jamila's head—he pulled because Paul couldn't deliver after he gave one million dollars up front."

"So he had him killed and what did you get out of this deal, Symone?" asked Oso, curious.

"My sister's life plus the one million dollars out of respect from Deoblow."

Oso looked around at his men. "Symone, you speak the truth. I had a talk with Deoblow already about this conversation we are having. I just needed to know that I can trust your word. In this line of business your word and money is all you have."

Symone saw herself killing Oso for playing mind games with her, but she knew that was the plug and she would never find prices like his. And Jamila would be hot if she crossed Oso.

"Symone, I have a new, but old drug I want you to push for me."

"And what is this drug, Oso?"

"I call it dog food. It's ten times more addictive than cocaine and comes in smaller packages. I'll give you, let's say, twenty kilos for sixty thousand dollars just to try it out, and if you like it we will talk greater numbers."

"And when can I receive this dog food?" replied Symone.

Oso snapped his fingers. One of his men picked up the duffle bag he had on the floor and passed it to him.

"Muscle, go lock the bar door and place the *close* sign in the window."

Oso opened the bag up, pulled a kilo out and placed it on the table. Masi and Symone watched Oso as he took a razor and cut the top of the kilo open, then took some out and placed it on a spoon. He pulled his lighter out and had the flame under the spoon. They watched as it started to bubble up. Once it cooled down a little, he took a needle and pulled the dog food that became a liquid inside the needle. He had one of his men come over, and he placed the needle in his veins. A few seconds later, the dude was leaning over from the drug.

"Symone, it's a high that they can't get away from. They need it like a newborn baby needs its mother."

"And how do I sack it up?" asked Symone.

"Just like this," Oso showed them how to sack it up in bundles, and the prices it was going by.

"Oso, I will have my guys give it a test run, and I will let you know from there."

"I hope to hear from you soon."

Oso got up and give Symone a kiss on the cheek before walking out with his guys.

Symone looked at the 20 kilos of dog food on the table in the bar, and put her *black-n-mild* out.

"Masi, get the bag and come on. We have work to do."

SAYNOMORE

Chapter 40

Slim was smoking a blunt when Symone called him.

"Hey, what's up, Symone?"

"We need to talk."

"Cool, when?"

"Tonight, and bring the two new guys—Iceman and Pete."

"What about Masi and Muscle?"

"No, I want them in the blind. I have a whole new crew for what I have in mind. Meet me at *Passions* at ten p.m."

"Sure, I'll be there."

"Slim, don't tell nobody about this meeting."

"I got you. I'll see you there."

Passions was jumping. There was a crowd of three hundred people. There was a new rap artist on stage strutting his stuff. Symone watched everything from her two-sided windows she had put in her office. Before long, Slim, Pistol and Iceman walked into her office. Without looking back, she said: "Take a seat." Symone turned around, walked to the table and sat down at the head.

"I will start the meeting up in a few seconds."

Slim looked at Symone, confused. That's when the door opened up, and Halo walked in with Lola. Symone watched as they took their seats.

"Everyone, this is Halo and Lola. Lola and Halo, this is Slim, Iceman and Pistol. I'm waiting on one more person to come, but he already told me he was going to be late. I called you all here because I'm about to open up a lot of new doors, and I want you to be a part of it. Everyone, Halo owns a jewelry store. He's been a licensed jeweler for over eight years now. Iceman here is known for getting people to have a very clear understanding with him. Our friend, Pistol, don't do too much talking and he means business. Our beautiful, lovely Lola is very loyal to me. She is my childhood friend who I had moved back up here just to be a part of this. I have a new, but old drug that is about to hit the streets of New York."

Symone placed a brick of dog food on the table in front of everyone.

"This right here is going to make us rich like never before. Ice-man, you will work the casino. Pistol, you have the strip club. Halo, we are going to open up a jewelry store downtown Manhattan. You will run it. Slim is my right-hand man. He will make my calls to ya. Lola will pick up the money and drop off the work. No slip-ups. Nobody—and nobody—outside the five of us should know about what we are doing."

That's when Perk-G walked in the door. All eyes were on him.

"Everyone, this is Perk-G, he is going to cook and sack up eve-rything for us. This is a six-man team. Let's get this money. We are not going to use the LaCross name. We are going to claim a name. I have one rule and one rule only—*you fuck up or cross me, you die*. That's all you need to remember. We start up everything this week."

Chapter 41

Four Months Later—

Iceman had the Ruby Red Casino on lock from selling dog food to the VIP. He had private rooms where girls would dance, fuck and suck on the clients to make them feel good after a night of gambling and a sack of *red flame*. He was raking in $100,000 to $150,000 every four days minus the gambling money. Lola would pick up the money and go to the diamond house strip club to see Pistol. Pistol had the baddest bitches in NYC dropping the ass at the diamond house. His girls would get their tricks drunk then hooked on the *red flames*. They would run their cards up, then empty their pockets out. On a good night, Lola would pick up $80,000. She would then drop the money off at Panache Fine Jewelry, where Halo would be waiting. He had the diamonds on lock in NYC from drug money to the press Symone was putting down. They were buying every jewelry store out, or bodies would be missing and found weeks later in the Hudson. Halo would make the runs to the bank. Perk-G had the workshop running smooth, two groups of females of three working 6-hour shifts in one of the Brownstones in Brooklyn. Lola would pick up and drop off to where she needed to. Iceman would get 6 kilos. Pistol would get 3 while Slim would always be ready for the next drop from Oso. Symone had it where there were two drop off spots, one for the dog food, the other for the powder. She had Masi picking up the powder, and Slim picking up the dog food. She still ran Queens while she had Lola overseeing everything else, checking in with her or Slim. Oso had what he wanted—his face in NYC, but Symone was the mask he was hiding behind. With his brother dead, Oso was the kingpin and Symone was his new hitta.

SAYNOMORE

Chapter 42

Joe sat down outside his bar, smoking his cigar and drinking his coffee early in the morning. He had four of his men outside with him.

"Joe, word on the streets is that there's a man named Iceman running a lot of drugs out the casino, and someone named Pistol doing the same thing with the strip club."

"I don't own the strip club or the casino no more, Bruno, so it's not my concern no more."

"I'm not saying it like that. What I'm saying is, maybe we can plug in with him and get a better deal than what we are getting now."

Joe laid the paper down and looked at Bruno.

"You have a point. Set it up and let's see where it goes."

Joe watched as Bruno walked off.

***

"Ma Rose, how long you been locked up for?"

"I been locked up, Jamila, for twenty-three years."

"If you don't mind me asking, what did you do?" asked Jamila.

"You know, Jamila, I read about you in the newspaper. You're the Queen Don. I remember the war with the Lenacci family. That was a bloody war. A lot of people died because of that war. At first, I thought, Jamila, you was going to be dead in the streets just like everyone else, but you surprised me. You surprised a lot of people."

Jamila looked at her as she talked.

"Jamila, I was you twenty-six years ago. My real name is Clyde-Ruth."

"Wait, you are Clyde-Ruth? I heard stories about you growing up," said Jamila.

"I'm sure you have."

"You had a pipeline from New York to Florida to GA. You moved drugs to over thirty states. You was the first female kingpin."

"I was, Jamila, I made more money than you could think of still to this day. I have hundreds of millions out there buried. Jamila, the point is to move like a ghost. I moved through the cracks for sixteen years before the FBI found out who I was. But by the time I knew about the case they had against me, I was getting locked up for murder and kidnapping. I was charged with the killing of Governor Clay's wife, brother, son and mother. The only deal was life in prison or face the death sentence. I had six of my top men telling on me, how I set it up step by step. So, I took the deal. It wasn't no point in fighting the case. I ain't want them to take the stand and bring more of my family down. So, I decided to take the fall for everyone."

"What about the men who told on you? What they get out the deal?" asked Jamila.

"They were given a new life. All of them were relocated abroad with new IDs."

"But with all the money you couldn't buy your way out of the situation this time?"

"No. What I ain't tell you, Jamila, was—one of my guys had on a wire when I called for the hit to be done. They got me dead to the wrong on everything. And the case with the FBI blew away when I never showed up for the drug deal. Seventy-two kilos of cocaine."

"So you just sit here and play chess now?"

"No, beautiful, I just learned how to move like a ghost again. What I like about you, Jamila—from the very first day you walked in here, you showed you wasn't the one to be fucked with. And when you got wet up on the yard, dear, you came back and took care of your business within forty-eight hours. I see now why Frankie took you under his wing."

"You know about that, Ms. Rose?" said Jamila.

"I told you I know a lot. I just don't speak on. You know the only thing you did, Jamila, that I ain't do is that you made friends with judges, DA's, police officers and lawyers, even the mayor. You opened a door that I never did, you showed your face to them and shook their hands."

Rose got up from the table. Jamila just watched her as she walked away. She understood what she was saying.

***

Iceman was looking at everyone gambling when Joe and two of his men walked into the casino. He walked down the stairs to meet them.

"Gentlemen, please follow me."

Symone had shown him pictures of Joe just in case a day like this happens. Once behind closed doors, Iceman took a seat at his desk.

"Joe Scott, Don of the Scott family, how can I help you?"

"I'm trying to do business, new business. It came to me that you are the person to talk to if I want this *red flame* that's been floating around here. How much are you asking for it?"

"Three kilos that will run you one hundred and eighty thousand dollars," said Iceman.

"No problem, when can I have it by?" asked Joe.

"When I get my money."

"I'll see you tomorrow. Tell Symone I like what she did with the place."

"I'll tell her."

Joe stuck his hand out for Iceman to shake it. Iceman got off the desk and shook his hand.

"Mr. Scott, please be here tomorrow by five-thirty p.m., and I'll have what you are asking for here for you."

"I'll see you, tomorrow, Iceman. I can find my way out."

Iceman watched as Joe and his two men left. He picked up the phone and called Symone.

"Hello."

"Hey, Joe just came by with two of his guys," said Iceman.

"What did he want?" asked Symone.

"The *red flame*."

"And what numbers was he talking?"

"I told him three for a hundred and eighty thousand dollars."

"And when do he want this by?"

"I told him tomorrow by five-thirty p.m."

"Okay. I'll be there when he comes. Make sure Lola makes the pick up on time. I don't want her there when he gets there. I don't want nobody to see her. She needs to be a ghost. I don't need nobody to know she is running for us."

"Okay. I got you, Symone."

Iceman hung up and looked out his office window at the poker table; he spotted a man who was cheating. He watched him a few more hands before he sent his men to get him.

"Hey, I'm sorry, but we need to stop the game for a second. Excuse me, sire, can you please come with us."

"Is there a problem?"

"Our boss would like to see you."

As he got up, he looked to his right where his friend was sitting. Iceman saw it all. He called one of his men and told him to also bring him to the man in green suit. When the two men from the poker table were brought to him, Iceman walked in the back room and looked at both of them sitting in two chairs.

"I hope ya are enjoying yourself."

"We are, sir."

"I wanted to ask you, how are you two enjoying the females and the drinks?"

"They are lovely."

"What is your name?" replied Iceman.

"Mike."

"Mike, I see you are the only one talking, but your friend here with the green suit is acting like he lost his tongue. Anyway, don't talk. Let me tell you two who I am. I am Iceman. I'm the manager of this casino, and I saw you two cheating at one of my tables."

They both looked scared when he said that. Iceman nodded, and one of his bodyguards pulled out his gun, looking at both of the culprits. Iceman looked at them. "You move, you die! Tie them both up to the chair."

"Listen, Mr. Iceman," the green-suit man finally spoke, "we are sorry. We really are. This will never happen again."

"I know it won't." Iceman walked away, picked up a chair and brought it close to them as one of his guards placed a towel over

Mike's face and held it tight while one of the other guards poured a bucket of water over his face. Mike was kicking, and his body was jumping as they poured the water over his face. Iceman told his guards to remove the towel. Mike gasped and wheezed, spitting out some of the water that had found its way down his throat. Iceman looked at the green-suit man, then said to his guards: "Give that nigga the same VIP treatment you gave Mike."

"Okay, boss," the guards chorused. They lost no time in waterboarding the green-suit man. He was squirming and kicking as they poured the water in his face.

After what seemed like an eternity, Iceman looked at them. "Remove the towel." Iceman scowled at the man, who was soaked to the core and trying to catch his breath.

"So here's the thing, I could kill ya or I can take one of your hands off, but you will not leave this casino unharmed. I can't let it get out that I had two motherfuckers stealing from me and ain't shit happened to them. But, I'm not going to kill you. I'll let both of ya live. Yo, J-Mitch, untie them."

Real Right—one of the guards—put the gun to their head. "Now both of you stick your fucking hands out, place them on the fucking arm of the chair." Iceman pulled his gun out and, with a cold smile, he shot both of them in the hand. They jumped back in the chair, screaming.

"Next time it will be your fucking life. Now get the fuck out of my casino." Iceman watched as they left, hiding their hands.

"Take them out the fucking back door."

***

Symone walked into Panache to see Halo. She walked to the back, where he was counting money.

"I see business is good with your press game. People can't help but to buy from us."

"So what brings you by?"

"I want a solid gold bar—two of them—and I want a chain made for me."

"I can get the gold bars in two days at the most, and what type of chain you want?" said Halo.

"I want blue and white diamonds VVF1, and I want them to spell out *Rose*."

"Who is Rose?"

Symone smiled at Halo. "I am Rose."

"Hmm. I like the sound of that, Symone."

Symone looked at one of the rings he had on the back shelf. It was a pinky ring with red, blue and white diamond. She picked it up and put it on.

"It fits you, Rose."

"It do, don't it. Halo, I'll be back in one week for my gold bar and chain."

When Symone walked out of Panache Fine Jewelry, she had Slim standing outside next to the limo. Once he saw her coming out, he opened the door for her. She stopped and looked at Slim.

"From here on out you will address me as Rose. Tomorrow I have a sit-down with Joe Scott. I want you and Pistol there."

"What's the sit-down about?" asked Slim.

"He wants three kilos of the *red flame*."

Symone reached in her bag, pulled out a *black-n-mild* and lowered her head to light it.

"Drop me off at *Jelani's* and go check out the other businesses, then go give me a count of the powder we have at the waste plant. I need to know all the numbers." Symone

"I'll have everything ready for you tomorrow, Rose."

"Good."

Chapter 43

Chief Tadem walked into his office and opened up his window to feel the morning breeze. He sat down behind his desk and turned his computer on. Before the computer could boot up, there was a knock at his door.

"Come in, Detective. It's nine a.m. and I ain't even start to drink my coffee or eat my bagel, so tell me what could I do for you."

"I want to open up a case on Symone LaCross. Before you say no, just hear what I have to say."

"Detective Green, the answer is no. I don't care what you have to say. Detective Boatman was killed working that case, shot six times and set on fire."

"Chief Tadem!"

"Detective, I said what I had to say."

"Damn, Chief, you act like Detective Boatman was a good cop, whereas he was mixed up in all that bullshit. What was it? *Two million in cash at his house and pictures of Red Invee standing over two dead bodies*. So, yea, he was killed, but those were the cards he dealt. He gambled with his life, and he paid for it with his life. And I got reason to fucking believe that Symone LaCross killed him. I heard the stories about her just like you, and we need to take her ass down before another cop ends up dead, or a DA with a missing head. We are cops. Our job is to protect the good and lock the bad guys up, Chief."

"You don't think I fucking know that, Detective? I know my job and you better learn your fucking place, Detective Green. You want to run a fucking case on Symone LaCross? You want to gamble with your life, then fuck it! Go ahead, super cop. Just make sure you tell your wife and daughter when to be ready when I come knocking at the fucking door, because I found your fucking body floating in the Hudson face down. You want your case, you got it. Now get the fuck out my office, Detective Green."

Detective Green walked out of Chief Tadem's office with a smile on his face. Symone was his victim, and he was going to bring the bitch down dead or alive.

***

Slim opened the limo door for Symone. Symone stepped out the limo and looked around. She had on a black mink coat that hung off her shoulders down to her calves. She was wearing a black and gray skin-tight dress with three-inch red bottom shoes on. Her midnight-black hair was in kinky twists, and she had on a pair of shades covering her face. When she walked in the casino, Real Right and J-Mitch met her in the entrance.

"Hello, Ms. LaCross, we came to walk you to the office."

Symone nodded at the both of them as she walked in the middle of them to Iceman's office. Once Symone was in the office, she looked at him. "Iceman?"

"Yes, Ms. LaCross."

"Why wasn't you at the door to meet me?"

"I was getting things ready for you in here, Ms. LaCross."

"You knew yesterday I was coming here, right?"

"Yes, I did," replied Iceman.

"Well, shit should have been ready. The next time you know I'm coming here, have your ass at the front door waiting for me!"

"It won't happen again, Ms. LaCross."

"Good, don't let it, and from here on out you will address me as Rose."

"Yes, Rose."

"Did Lola bring the three kilos of *red flame*?"

"Yea, she did about two hours ago."

"Slim, can you go fix me something to drink? No ice or brown. Just make it Cîroc Apple."

"Okay, Rose," Slim replied.

"J-Mitch, I want you and Real Right downstairs when Joe Scott walk in here."

"Yes, Rose"

Symone took her coat off and laid it on the back of the chair, then sat down.

"Iceman, so tell me, how is business going?"

"Good like always. I have the girls doing their thing. Everything is going like bread and butter, nice and smooth."

"Good, that's what I like to hear. So I heard the story, how you got this place. Iceman, one thing we don't do in the Mafia is, talk about our past actions."

Iceman nodded.

Symone looked up on the camera and saw Joe Scott and three of his men walking in the casino with J-Mitch and Real Right on their sides, bringing them to the office. Slim passed Symone her drink. She took a sip, as she watched them on camera walking up to the office doors. Joe was shocked when he saw Symone sitting at the table. Symone got up and walked up to him and shook his hand.

"Joe, I believe the last time I saw you was at Paul's burial."

"You are right about that, Symone."

"Please call me Rose. So I was told you wanted three kilos of *red flame*."

"Yea, that's right, I do. It's sweeping through the streets."

"That's hundred percent pure."

Joe picked up the bag he'd brought, laid it on the table and started pulling money out of it.

"Joe, stop, there's no need for you to do that. Slim, place the kilos of *red flame* on the table. Mr. Scott, take these kilos as a gift from me to you and if you like how it moves in the streets, then I will be ready for you to shop with me."

"Rose, you know we got off on a wrong start, but it's always time to make a new beginning."

"You are right, Mr. Scott, so I'm opening up that door today with you."

"So, Rose, should we have a drink to a new friendship?" asked Joe.

"I think we should."

Iceman watched as they talked for the next thirty minutes about other business in the future before walking them out the casino doors.

SAYNOMORE

Chapter 44

Jamila sat down at the table with Amber as they watched the news early that morning.

"Jamila, it's going on three years you been locked up.Do you think everything is going to be the same when you go home?"

"I know a lot has changed, Amber, but all my numbers are the same from all my businesses. There have not been a war in almost a year, and Lorenzo is watching over things for me from another point of view. I am the Queen, and everyone knows that. So I know everything will be the same how I left it."

"Hello, ladies."

"Good morning, Ms. Rose."

"So what was the conversation about you two were just having before I walked up?"

"Amber asked me do I think everything will be the same when I go home, and I do think everything will be the same when I go home."

"Jamila, do you think everything will be the same?"

"Yes I do."

"Hmmm."

"Why you say *hmmm*, Ms. Rose?"

"Because when one king falls, another always rises. It's been that way since the beginning of time. Jamila, you have a very strong name in the streets, but there will always be someone trying to step over your name to make their own. You told me about Lorenzo, but you never told me exactly why you wanted him all the way out the picture."

"Because the role he plays is just as big as mine, and I don't want him in here with me, so I want him watching over everything until I come home, but from behind the scene."

"Beautiful, you don't think he might have felt some kind of way that you ain't trust him to be the face till you come home.You have someone who's been loyal to you from day one before you knew you had a sister. And Jamila, let's face the facts, you overlooked him and crowned your sister.He might not have said nothing out of respect, but I'm sure he didn't like that, plus I heard there is a new king coming up in the streets right now that's in downtown Manhattan and Brooklyn that calls herself Rose, and she's flooding the streets with da dog food she calls *red flame*. She ain't reached Queens, but it's only a matter of time before she crosses over."

Amber glanced at Jamila and Ms. Rose.

"There's two families that runs Brooklyn and Manhattan already, so if they are letting this Rose person push on their streets and take food out of their mouths, that's on them. Facts!" exclaimed Jamila.

"You make a really good point, Jamila, but just think about this. How do you know this person doesn't have the press on both families over Brooklyn and Manhattan?" Ms. Rose questioned. "Jamila, Frankie will have you believing that the head don has the last word, which is so not true because if that was true, Tony would still be here. He had the people's respect, but not their love, because if he had their love, you would've been dead because family can't take on the Mafia, and he was the boss of all bosses."

Jamila asked out of curiosity. "So what should I do, Ms. Rose?"

"I just told you what you should do. Read between the lines because someone else should be wearing the crown while you are in here."

Jamila knew what Ms. Rose was saying was right, and she needed to get in touch with Lorenzo because he should be the king right now.

Chapter 45

Passions was jumping. People were dancing on stage. The DJ was playing 2-Pac's *Me and My Girlfriend* for throwback Thursday. Symone strutted inside *Passions* with Masi and Muscle in tow.

The DJ saw her walk in. "Big shout to Symone aka Rose in the building!"

Symone pointed over at the DJ and nodded in his direction. When Symone opened her office door, Lorenzo was standing there in a white suit and matching colored shoes while smoking a cigar. His hair was in curls, and he had diamond earrings in both ears.

"Lorenzo, how long you been here for? I didn't even know you was here," Symone stated.

"Masi, Muscle, you two watch da floor for a little while—I need to talk to Symone in private," Lorenzo said, then watched as the two made an exit before speaking.

"Symone, I'm not going to act like I'm happy to see you because I'm not. However, I respect the fact you still took care of the business. But, along your part to becoming this Rose, you forgot that you are not the Queen and you do not own any keys to the city. You was just holding the keys, which I'm here to take back." Lorenzo's voice was stern.

"What do you mean take them back? Red Invee gave me the crown until she comes home and she just took it back. Your part in the LaCross family just went on pause, Lorenzo."

Lorenzo walked up to Symone until he was face to face with her. "Loyalty, trust, and honor you threw out da window when you started pushing your dog food. What you call it? *Red flame*, Symone?" he asked sarcastically. "Mafia rules, *not trappin' on no one's turf*. You're not bigger than the mob. I wasn't in the picture, but I got the phone calls, and that's what you call mob ties. Jamila called me last night. It's over, Symone."

Lorenzo walked to the back-office door and opened it. Symone looked and saw Tasha, Crystal, Masi, Muscle and four more members of the LaCross family as they walked inside the door. They all stood behind Lorenzo. Symone stared into their eyes and knew they would kill her if she tried anything.

"Tasha, Crystal, go ahead," Lorenzo said.

They both walked up to Symone. Tasha said to her: "Lemme get that chain off your neck." Symone looked at her, then cast a glance at Crystal.

Crystal pulled her gun out. "Don't let her ask again."

"Symone, here's the rule—" Lorenzo began once Symone let Tasha remove the chain from her neck. "You have seventy-two hours to move all your things out of Jamila's Brownstone, *Jelani's*, the waste plant and *Destiny's*. You are no longer allowed to use the LaCross family name. You can't set up nothing in Queens. Queens is no longer your home. Slim Boogie has twenty-four hours from tonight to have our family diamond chain back to me in my possession." Lorenzo paused for a moment, eyeing Symone distastefully. Then he went on with Red Invee's decree:

"Now, this is what your sister is going to do for you— she's going to let you live, she's going to give you her blessings to start your own family. Nobody can touch you. You're a made woman right now. You used the LaCross family name to get the strip club and to get the casino, so you owe twenty-five percent of what the casino is worth and the strip club whenever it's paid off. I must stress one thing finally—Red Invee breaks all ties with you."

Symone didn't respond. She stared into everyone's eyes once more before walking out the door.

"Symone!" Lorenzo called out to her, stopping her in her tracks. "If I don't have Slim's chain within twenty-four hours, his body will end up floating in the Hudson River." Symone didn't bother responding to his threat. She just walked out of the room.

Lorenzo glanced at everyone in the office. "If you see her in Queens, kill her before she kills you because this ain't going to go the way Red Invee thinks it's going to go. I can see it in her eyes."

Symone walked out of *Passions* with rage in her eyes and hopped in her BMW. 50 Cent's *When It Rains It Pours* was playing from her sound system. All she could think about was killing Lorenzo.

She drove around Queens for an hour before finding herself parked in front of *Jelani's*. With tears in her eyes, she opened the door, as flashbacks of all the things she had done for the LaCross Family ran through her mind.

She pulled both of her guns out, got out of the car, and immediately began shooting up the spot. Windows shattered and gunshots echoed loudly. Symone slowly walked inside the building, placed both of her guns down on the desk, and looked around the place one last time. Moments later, she climbed back in her car and drove off.

SAYNOMORE

Chapter 46

Lorenzo walked through the broken glass window at *Jelani's*. Masi handed him two pistols.

"Lorenzo, what you think this mean?" Masi began speaking. "I saw she had the same exact menacing look she had in her eyes last night."

"Hold on, Masi, my phone is going off." Lorenzo interrupted. "Hello," Lorenzo pressed one on the phone to accept the phone call from Jamila. "We have a problem."

"I'm listening, Lorenzo," Jamila spoke calmly.

"Look, I told her everything you told me to tell her word for word. I got the chain last night, and this morning I got both guns from her after she shot up *Jelani's*. She left both guns on the front desk."

"Lorenzo, from this point on, she's nothing to me. Handle your business. Blood ain't thicker than the Mafia, copy?" Jamila hung up.

"What she say?" Masi asked out of curiosity.

"Kill her," Lorenzo calmly replied.

"I'ma take care of that now, Lorenzo."

"A'ight, get Muscle and three more men, but remember, she's not gonna second guess about killing you," Lorenzo stated seriously.

Lorenzo watched as Masi got in the black SUV, gun in hand as he pulled off.

***

"Symone, you know Jamila's going to send Lorenzo after us, right?" Slim uttered.

"Well, let 'em come. Iceman got Real Right, J-Mitch, and a few more men holding the casino down."

"I told Pistol what the move was, so he gotta few guys with him. Perk-G and Lola are in the cut, but I already informed the both of them as well."

"Slim, when Crystal pulled that gun out on me, I regretted everything I've done for the family," Symone spoke sternly. "Come on, Slim, let's go get something to eat."

While the two were walking down the stairs from the Brownstone, there were two black SUV's parked down the block, observing them.

"Muscle, you're ready?" questioned Masi.

"Yea, let's get this shit over and done with," Muscle replied.

"Symone, do you see them SUV's?" Slim asked

"Yeah. Oh shit! Slim, it's a hit!" As soon as Symone answered, the two SUV's pulled off with guns hanging out of the windows, pointing in Symone and Slim's direction. Symone and Slim leaped from the steps, sprinting to the side of the building.

Muscle began dumping a Mac-11 out of the window at the trucks, as Slim tripped over a broken bike. Symone also turned around and returned fire from behind a garbage dumpster.

"Slim, hurry, get up!" Symone managed to shout out.

Bullets were flying both ways. Symone watched as bullets ripped through Slim's body while he was getting up. She observed two men jump out of the vehicle as Slim hit the ground. Symone raised both of her guns and sprinted towards the SUV, shooting. She shot one of the guys in the head, and shot the other one in the side. When Muscle pulled his gun in finally, Masi started shooting at Symone.

"You want to kill me, Masi? Fuck you, pussy. I ain't running. I'm right here!" Symone continued firing until one of the bullets caught Masi in the hand, forcing him to drop his weapon.

Muscle hit the side of the SUV. "Come on, let's get tha fuck outta here now!" he said.

Symone watched the vehicles pull off while yelling "I'ma kill every one of you motherfuckers on God!" She ran back over to Slim who was desperately trying to catch his breath as blood flowed out of his mouth.

"Si—Symone—I can't—breath," Slim somehow managed to say.

"Slim, don't worry. I'ma get you some help. Just hold on!"

Symone saw flashing lights coming down the block. She picked up Slim's guns and looked at him pitifully. His last word before he passed out was: "Run". Symone glanced at the guy she shot in the side where he was trying to get up. He looked up at her as she aimed her gun at him.

"Lorenzo called the hit and he got yo' fuck ass killed, nigga!" Symone spat, then put two shots in his head, sprinting back into an alley before the police arrived at the scene.

SAYNOMORE

Chapter 48

Symone walked into Southside Hospital. She strutted towards the doctor's office.

"Ms. Symone, have a seat," the doctor instructed.

"Doc, just lay it on me, no cuts," insisted Symone.

"He was brought here yesterday, and he has lost an enormous amount of blood. He already done had two blood transfusions, so as of now we do not know if he's going to make it, and I can't take him to the pink houses because he's in bad shape." The doctor paused for a moment, then his voice turned somber as he continued. "Also, there's a seventy percent chance that he may not make it. He was shot three times. Let me show you something," the doctor put Slim's X-rays onto the projector screen.

"You see right here, Symone, the bullet hit his lung, wherein if he hadn't arrived here in the time that he did, he probably wouldn't be alive as of now. He's fighting for his life right now dramatically."

Upon hearing the disturbing news, Symone bit down on her bottom lip. "Doc, I have a hundred thousand dollars for you. Just make sure he survives. Doc, hear me carefully—I need this man in my life like my heart beat."

"I will do my best, Symone."

"That's all I'm asking you to do for me, Doc," Symone replied, then stood and walked out of the doctor's office.

Once she was in her car, she called Halo and told him to have everyone meet her at the casino at 9 p.m., and she also wanted the casino closed tonight.

***

Lorenzo was looking at Masi and Muscle, as he sat behind his desk with his index finger touching his temple.

"So lemme get this correct—it was five of you total in two SUV's," Lorenzo began addressing the two. "Masi, you come back with a gunshot in your fucking hand and Muscle you shot a Mac-

11. No, lemme say it this way—You empty the clip and hit Slim. Is he dead?"

"I don't know," Muscle answered honestly.

"But what you do know is that there's two more dead LaCross family members that I have to let Red Invee know about! Look, both of you go post up at *Destiny's* and be ready because she's coming back. If you know like I know, don't let her take you alive because it will be a death you will suffer from before you die!"

***

Symone walked into the House of Diamonds strip club, where Lola had been waiting on her arrival. She walked into the back office.

"Hey, Rose, I heard about Slim," Lola said.

"Lola, he's a soldier. He'll be just fine, but I need you more than anybody right now."

"Girl, yo' know I'm down for you, facts! What you need for me to do?" Lola asked.

"I need you to be somebody else for me."

"Who you need me to be?" Lola questioned curiously.

"Sony Smith," Rose answered. "I need for you to look your best at all times, always have on a suit. I need for you to look professional at all times. I don't want you to give nobody a conversation. Don't be rude, but don't be a push over neither. Sex is going to come with what I'm asking of you to do. Here, take this picture because this is the man whom I need you to hook up with."

"And once I get him then what?" Lola asked, still confused a little.

"Put this in his drink. Once he is asleep, call me," Symone instructed, then jotted down the address that she needed Lola to stay at. "Lola, from this point on, I don't want you at the casino nor this damn strip club or Fine Jewelry. I have something for you from Halo." Lola stared at Symone as she reached into her bag. Symone pulled out three black boxes and placed them on the table. She opened all three boxes while Lola looked at the yellow diamond chain, yellow diamond earrings and yellow diamond bracelet.

"You like them?" Symone asked.

"God, they are beautiful, Symone!" exclaimed Lola.

"And they are going to look wonderful on you," said Symone. "Here is four thousand dollars for you. I don't want you to be in contact with no one until this job is complete. Lola, look at me, I want you to remember this because it's going to be your life or his." Lola nodded at Symone's last words.

Symone kissed her on the left cheek and handed her a set of car keys. "There's a white Lexus outside. From here on out, that is what you will drive. I don't need nobody to recognize you. Call me whenever you ready to see me but not before then. Also, one more thing, I want you to eat at this address Friday night."

Symone handed her a card, then walked off. Lola looked at the card before putting it in her pocket.

***

Iceman was waiting on Symone when she walked through the doors of the casino.

"How you doing, Rose?" Iceman said.

"I'm fine. Is everyone here already?" Symone asked.

"Yea, everyone is upstairs waiting on you."

"Good, let's not keep them waiting."

Symone walked in the doors and saw Pistol, Perk-G, Halo, Real Right, J-Mitch, Man, and BR seating at the table.

"Before anyone asks me, Slim is in ICU. He's a soldier so he's going to pull through. With that being said, Red Invee feels as though I crossed her or wasn't loyal to her because I ain't let her eat at this table with ya. I was a part of the LaCross family for four years, so I know how they move. Right now they are waiting on us to make a move, but we are not. Yesterday I killed two of their men, but their blood ain't the blood I want. I want the king's blood! I want to hit them where it hurts the most, then I want the Queen, and from here on out we're our own family." Symone paused for a moment. Then, with a deadly serious look in her eyes she went on:

"We are the Rose Family. We are gonna take what the fuck we want, set up shop, we do what the fuck we want and break the rules when we want. They talk about making the streets hot. We gon' make them blazing. Pistol, I want eyes on everyone that comes in the House of Diamonds. I want a camera at every entrance. Man, I want you at the front door.BR, I want you on the floor. Real Right, the same thing with you—I want you also at the front door. J-Mitch, I want you on the floor. Halo, I'll be with you at Panache Fine. I don't want nobody to reach out Lola at all. Perk-G, nobody knows about you so I need you to keep making up the kilos of *red flame* because that's where most of our money is coming from." Symone finished giving commands, then walked to the bar and retrieved a bottle of Cîroc with eight shot glasses. She poured everyone a shot. "To the Rose Family." At that moment, everyone at one time said: "To the Rose Family!"

Chapter 49

Jamila watched as Ms. Rose walked into her cell. She walked down the stairs to her cell where she knocked twice before entering.

"Jamila, what can I do for you?" asked Ms. Rose.

"Ms. Rose, when I first started my family, Frankie told me that sometimes you have to kill family members," Jamila stated. "I green-lighted Lorenzo to kill my little sister, but his shooters missed the shot and two of my soldiers took the fall," she revealed. "I know she's gonna come back." Jamila paused for a few seconds.

"What is your biggest fear?" Ms. Rose curiously asked.

"She can't get to me, so she gon' try to kill Lorenzo," Jamila replied. "I know that's what she's up to because it's been a week and she hasn't struck back yet. Lorenzo has seven million in a black duffle bag Symone sent to him."

"And what exactly is that for?"

"The twenty-five percent from the casino and strip club."

"If I was your sister, I would wait on the right time. And to be honest, I think that it's time that you face the fact, Jamila, that you no longer have a sister. You have a blood line with two sisters and one city. From what I'm told, she has a few very loyal soldiers. Just ask yourself this: if she had you down bad with a gun to your face, would she see her father's child or would she see her as an enemy? She's not that little girl you took in four years ago. She's a killer now." Without uttering another word, Jamila licked her lips and walked out of Ms. Rose's cell.

Jamila walked over to the pay phone and dialed Lorenzo's number.

"Hello," he spoke into the receiver.

"What's up, Lorenzo?"

"Nothing. How's things with you?"

"I'm good. It's only a few more months left, nine with good time, but listen—I know why she ain't try nothing yet."

"And why you think she ain't tried nothin' yet?" questioned a curious Lorenzo.

Before responding, Jamila let out a slight sigh. "Because she's coming after you."

"Shid, you made the call against her, so she should be coming after you," Lorenzo shot back. "I'm not worried about her, but I'll keep an eye out," he added.

"Okay. What are you doin'?"

"I'm about to walk into *Destiny's.*"

"Well, okay, I'll call you sometime later this week," stated Jamila.

"A'ight, Jamila, keep your head up in there."

"Trust me, I will." Jamila hung up, hoping Lorenzo took heed to what she had told him and stayed vigilant.

***

Lorenzo had Masi and Muscle waiting on him at *Destiny's*.

"So how's business going?" he asked as soon as he walked inside.

"Good. Here's the deposits for the week."

"How much is it?"

"Eighty-eight hundred."

Before Lorenzo could respond, his attention was captured by a light-skinned female seated at a table occupied by a laptop. She was so beautiful that he couldn't help but lock in on her. Her complexion was honey brown. She had long, blond hair. She was wearing a black suit with gray pinstripes along with a pair of open-toe Red Bottoms. Her fingernails—as well as toenails—were painted white. She had on several gaudy jewelry pieces, which was courtesy of Symone. Lorenzo watched her intensively as she sipped on her morning coffee.

"Look, Masi, take these deposits back and I'll get it from you in a little while," Lorenzo instructed.

"Yo, trust me, Lorenzo, she's not even worth it. Shorty already done blew me and Muscle off twice," Masi revealed.

"See, that's the thing. I'm not you or Muscle!" Lorenzo took the opportunity and walked over to the table where the lady was seated.

"Excuse me," Lorenzo spoke, getting Sony's attention. She glanced up, making eye contact with his hazel eyes. "Lorenzo," he introduced himself, extending his hand for a more proper greeting.

"Hi, Lorenzo, nice to meet you. Sony Smith," she introduced herself, then she offered her hand to accept his gesture.

"Do you mind if I sit with you, Mrs. Smith?"

"No, I don't mind and it's just Smith, I'm not married."

"If you don't mind me asking, what are you workin' on?" Lorenzo questioned as he took a seat across from Sony.

"Nothing, I was just emailing my sister."

"Listen, I'm not gon' front, Sony, you beautiful. I couldn't help but stop and talk to you."

"Well, thank you, Lorenzo!" she blushed. "I noticed you have on a power suit. If you don't mind me asking, exactly what it is that you do for a living?"

"Well, I'm part owner of this hotel that you're staying at."

"You own this hotel?" Sony asked in disbelief as Lorenzo let out a slight chuckle.

"Part owner," he clarified. "So what is it you do for a living?" he asked.

"Web design for the NFL and NBA. I work for a private company."

"Smart, beautiful and bold, damn, how can I get your number?" This time Sony let out a chuckle at Lorenzo.

"Are you going to be a stalker if I don't call or text you right back, Mr. Lorenzo?"

"Nah, no worries 'bout that, black queen."

"Well then, sure, you can have my number. Where's your phone at?" she asked.

Lorenzo smiled as he handed his phone to Sony. He watched as she put her number into his phone.

"So, when are you going to call me?" he asked excitedly.

"How does this weekend sound?"

"Sounds good to me."

"Cool, I'll call you then," Sony replied, then watched as Lorenzo walked out to where Masi and Muscle were waiting on him. Lorenzo turned around to see Sony staring at him before he made his departure.

Chapter 50

Joe Scott was seated out front of his bar with a few of his men when a black Hummer limousine pulled up. He watched as the driver walked around to the back passenger door and opened it. He saw Iceman and Rose step out of the limo. Symone had a new look to her; she looked like a model. Joe stood up and walked to meet her.

"Rose, what do I owe the honor of this visit?"

"Just came to see how you're enjoying *red flame*," answered Rose.

"I'm glad that you bring that up because I wanted to talk more business with you about that. Please come have a seat with me," Joe insisted, as he walked over to a table and pulled out a chair for Rose to sit.

"So, Mr. Scott, tell me about the business that you want to do with me."

"Rose, you're doing business in Brooklyn and my family runs Brooklyn, but I want us to come to an understanding, where maybe we can wash each other hands," Joe suggested.

"I'm listening."

"Allow me to buy my kilos from you for twenty-one thousand a pop and you can make Brooklyn your second home."

"Mr. Scott, you know we got off on the wrong foot so I will do that for you and you will become one of my allies, she suggested.

"So you want me to be a part of the LaCross family?"

"No, I've recently started my own family, the Rose family, so do we have a deal?" Joe Scott stared at Symone, trying to read her, then he shook her hand, which solidified them as allies.

"We have a deal, Ms. Rose," he confirmed.

Symone waved Iceman over to them, where he hurried over and handed her a bag. She pulled out a red glass rose, where on the petals read: *loyalty, respect, and honor.*

"Mr. Scott, let today begin a beautiful friendship and from this day forward, the Rose family will always have your back," said Symone.

"Likewise, Rose."

Symone got up and gave Joe Scott a hug and kiss on the left cheek before strutting away. Joe Scott watched the limousine pull off. Meanwhile, Detective Green was seated in a navy-blue car down the street, taking pictures. He had been following Symone for the last three days. He had a long-distance microphone so he could hear their conversation, where he had just learned that Symone was Rose, whom just so happens has her own family now. Within the past three days he'd taken an ample amount of photos of not only Symone, but of Halo, Iceman, Pistol, Man, BR, and Perk-G. He had a wall with all their pictures on it, and Rose was at the top of the pyramids. The only question he had was, *why she wasn't a part of the LaCross family anymore*? It was one of the most powerful families in NYC, but he also knew that Lorenzo was back in the picture and he'd been missing for three and a half years. Detective Green pulled off to head back to the police station to develop the pictures, and to also let Chief Tadem know Symone Rose and Joe Scott were now allies.

Mob Ties 4

Chapter 51

Lorenzo stared out of the window of the limo as he rode in the back seat to go see Oso. He glanced and saw his phone was going off. "Hello."

"Yo, it's Masi. What's up?"

"I just got word that Symone was talking to Joe Soctt yesterday."

"Do you know about what?" Masi asked.

"No, but she gave him a red rose and before she left their meeting, she gave him a hug and kiss on the cheek, but that's not all. I was told she started her own family."

"Do you know where she posted up at?"

"She might be in Brooklyn, I'm not sure."

"I know why she went to see him. She just made him an ally," Masi said.

"This is what I want you to do. You, Muscle, Tasha, and Dro, go pay Mr. Scott a visit and if what you are saying is true, kill him," Lorenzo ordered. "Call me back and lemme know what he say," he added.

"Copy," Masi replied. Lorenzo hung up as the limo was pulling up to the country club where he was meeting Oso.

Once he stepped out of the limo, he saw Oso standing outside in some white dress pants, white shoes, a pink dress shirt with a white and pink hat. He was also wearing a gold chain with a cross medallion. He was smoking a cigar. He smiled when he spotted Lorenzo step out of the limousine.

"Lorenzo, I'm so glad you made it. Come, let's go talk and have a drink," Oso insisted.

"So, tell me, how's Red Invee doing?"

"Actually she's doing good with her good time. She might be home, she says, within the next nine months."

"Listen, Lorenzo, I called you here to see if I can drop a bigger shipment on you."

"How big are we talking?"

"Like three hundred more kilos. Do you think you can handle that much more?"

"With no problem, but what are the prices you're talking?" Lorenzo asked.

"I'll cut the prices from what you are paying now by ten percent. How that sounds?"

"I'll say let's drink to that, Oso!" exclaimed Lorenzo.

Oso smiled, picked up a bottle of Brandy and poured both of them a stiff shot. The two tapped their glasses before taking their shots.

"To new business!" Oso toasted.

"To new business," Lorenzo repeated.

***

Tasha walked into Joe Scott's bar with Masi, Muscle, and Dro following her. Joe emerged from the back with four of his men.

"How may I help you?" Joe Scott asked calmly.

"We came to find out some facts behind a rumor that came across our table," replied Tasha.

"And just who are you, ma'am?"

"Tasha LaCross."

"Alright then, Ms. Tasha LaCross, entertain me by telling me exactly what is the rumor that has come across the table."

"That you and Symone Rose are now allies," Tasha answered.

Before responding, Joe reached inside his pocket, retrieved a lighter and lit a cigar. "Tasha, yes, the rumor that has come across your table is one hundred percent true. The Rose family home is now in Brooklyn," he confirmed.

Masi scanned around the bar at everyone he knew, and sensed that it was no-win situation.

"Thank you, Mr. Scott, for the information. That's all Lorenzo wanted to know. You have a good day," said Masi. They all turned and exited as quickly as they all had come.

Joe Scott watched as the family walked out of his bar.

"You think they'll try something, Joe?" one of Joe Scott's men questioned.

"I highly doubt it. I think they know it's a new rising Queen that's emerging who's deadlier than Red Invee, and there's not anything they can do to stop it, Freddie. And when Rose wins, we win. Come on, let's get outta here. I have to contact Rose to let her know that we had visitors asking about our new friendship."

Chapter 52

Three days later, Sony was seated at a restaurant table. She was eating and sipping on a glass of wine, enjoying her evening alone. Lorenzo walked over to the second range floor reel of the restaurant from the VIP seats, and stared down on everyone until his eyes finally locked in on Sony. He just stood there for a few minutes, taking in her beauty. He pulled out his phone and called her. Sony glanced at her phone and smiled. Lorenzo saw the look on her face as she smiled.

"Well, hello, Mr. Lorenzo," she answered in a joyful manner.

"Hello, beautiful. How are you this lovely evening?"

"I'm good, just enjoying a very good, but very expensive dinner by myself, she replied.

"Would you like some company?"

"First of all, you don't even know where I'm at. I could be thirty minutes away from you, sir."

"Yeah, you could be or you could be thirty seconds away from me," he stated calmly.

"Okay, sure, I'm at a restaurant called *Jelani's* in Queens."

"I'm familiar with the spot. I'll see you in a few."

"I'll be here waiting on you, Mr. Lorenzo."

"Great! I'm on my way to you now, beautiful," Lorenzo replied.

Sony was still eating when Lorenzo walked up behind her. "Hello, beautiful."

"How did you get here so fast? Lorenzo, don't let me find out you're following me!" Sony said in amazement.

"Nah, I'm not following you, but the way you're looking right now—I might start!"

"Whatever, Lorenzo," she smiled at his charm.

"Damn, can I have a hug?"

Sony stuck out her lips and rolled her eyes back. "I guess you can." Lorenzo smiled as she stood, allowing them to embrace each other.

"Damn, you smell wonderful and your body is charmingly soft!" Lorenzo complimented.

"Well, thank you, handsome!" she flirted. "So, how did you get here so fast?" she asked.

"Let's sit and I'll tell you," Lorenzo insisted, and the two took their seats.

"I'm waiting."

"Well, long story short," he paused, "I'm also part owner of this restaurant as well," he revealed.

"You are doing way too much, Lorenzo, and I don't believe you," Sony said, not convinced.

"Now, why would I lie to you?" Lorenzo glanced over and saw a waiter coming out of the kitchen and called her over to their table as Sony just sat and watched everything.

"Yes, Mr. LaCross?"

"Have someone bring me two meals of the day and a bottle of Ace of Spades upstairs to my office right away. Wrap this meal up and bring it to my office as well."

"Yes, sir."

"Thank you." Lorenzo reached over the table, grabbed Sony's hand and got up from the table, then guided her over to the elevator that led to the office on the second range.

"Lorenzo, I want to just apologize for saying I didn't believe you," Sony said.

Lorenzo didn't respond. He just stared into her eyes as they were on the elevator, then he pulled her closely to him and kissed her on the forehead. She looked up at him and placed her hand on his chin, then pulled his face to hers. Sony began kissing Lorenzo as he returned the welcoming gesture until the elevator finally stopped on the second floor.

"Come in, Sony, my office is this way," Lorenzo said.

When they made it to his office and walked inside, Sony couldn't believe how beautiful his office was. She couldn't help but to look around. When she glanced over to her right, she spotted a picture of Jamila and Symone on the wall. Sony couldn't help but look at them, walking closer to the picture. Lorenzo walked up behind her.

"Lorenzo, who are they?" she asked, as if she didn't already know the answer.

"That's Jamila LaCross—the Queen of the city. And that's her little sister—Symone. Lemme show you something." He led her over to the sliding glass doors. "Sony, some nights I'll come out here and just look out at the city. It be so peaceful."

"And it looks so peaceful up here, Lorenzo, plus the view is amazing!" exclaimed Sony.

Lorenzo turned around to see the waitress bring their food into the office.

"Come on, our food is here," he told Sony. She glanced one more time out at the city before walking off to the table behind Lorenzo.

***

Symone was seated behind her desk, looking at the two gold bars Halo had got for her. She had her and Slim Boogie's name's engraved in both of them because the two had started this family together. The gold bars represented their foundation. Trust, loyalty, and respect was as solid and pure as gold. Symone had gone to see Slim. He was doing much better. She had him moved to a private hospital in Long Island. The doctor had informed her that within the next few weeks, Slim should be around sixty-five percent strong. The doctor had done his part by making sure that Slim survived and was taken care of. Iceman made all the changes Symone asked for within the casino, and so did Pistol. Oso had his people dropping right off to Perk-G. Now the money was coming in nice and smooth. Symone had to get two more Brownstones. One of the Brownstones served as a place where they made their kilos. The other was used for stashing the money. Halo had started dealing with A-list celebrities on custom-made jewelry. Everything was working out the way Symone had expected. Joe Scott had told her about the visitors he had that had stopped by his establishment. She was worried about the threats. She wanted to hit them where it hurt the most, and she was just waiting on that phone call because she had a bullet with

Lorenzo's name on it. She couldn't wait to use that bullet. Symone was the new rising Queen, and she was going to face Red Invee head-on over the crown.

Chapter 53

Chief Tadem walked to his office to see Detective Green leaning against the wall next to the office door. With a smile on his face, Detective Green was holding two cups of coffee and a yellow file in his hand. Chief Tadem walked up to him and took a cup of coffee out of his hand.

"So, are you going to tell me exactly why you're smiling from ear to ear?" Chief Tadem asked out of curiosity.

"Once we get into your office, I sure will," Detective Green happily replied. Chief Tadem didn't bother to respond; he just sauntered into his office, walked over and opened his window, then sat at his desk.

"Okay, now tell me what you got, Detective Green."

"Well, for starters, Symone is no longer a part of the LaCross family."

"And how do you know this, Detective?" questioned Chief Tadem.

"I followed her to Joe Scott's bar, and she actually said it herself, listen—" Detective Green pulled out the tape recorder that he had tucked away in his jacket.

Chief Tadem sat and listened to the whole recording. "So, she's now allies with Joe Scott?"

"That's not all, Chief. About two weeks ago, there was a shooting in Brooklyn where two people were murdered and one shot in the chest. Well, the one that was shot in the chest—his name's Lamar Otis aka Slim Boogie. He's Symone Rose's second-in-command. Thus, I have good reasons to believe that Symone Rose murdered the other two men in the alleyway in Brooklyn. So, this is what I do know—Symone Rose has Iceman, J-Mitch, Man, and BR at the casino. Here are pictures of all of them. All of their government names are on the photos of all of them. Now, at the House of Diamonds strip club she has Pistol, No Dee, Real Right, and A-Dog. Here goes their photos with their government names—"

Detective Green handed Chief Tadem the photos. "Now, here are photos of Halo, whom she keeps at a jewelry shop called

Panache Fine in downtown Manhattan. From what I can tell, that's the main place she be at most of the time. However, I'm still trying to find out the identity of these two people that are standing next to her. I couldn't get a picture of their faces, but you can tell that it's a female and guy. Just don't know who."

"Detective Green, I see that you've been doing your homework and getting right down to it, but I'm asking you to leave this investigation alone," Chief Tadem ordered.

"Not until I have Symone Rose's ass in an eight-by-ten cell!" Detective Green snapped back.

"Well, good luck, Detective." Chief Tadem handed him back the pictures with the files. "Keep me posted in your investigation."

"Will do, sir," Detective Green replied, then got up and walked out of Chief Tadem's office. Chief Tadem knew Detective Green was over his head, and a horrible death was in his future.

Chapter 54

Symone was in the back of a BMW as Pistol chauffeured her around Queens.

"Rose, what are we looking for?" questioned Pistol.

"Oh, nothing, I just wanted to ride through Queens," she replied. "Pistol, I'm thinking about opening up a nightclub," she added.

"Where at?"

"Brooklyn," she replied. "What! I know I ain't trippin! Damn, it feels good when the rabbit got the gun," Symone said excitedly.

"Rose, what you see?"

"Tasha's ass. You see her over there with her little boy? That's the bitch who pulled up on me with Crystal who had a bitch down bad!" Symone angrily explained.

"Shid, what you wanna do, bag two bodies?"

"Bad timing, it's too many people here right now."

"Shorty, look like she going into that dollar store over there," said Pistol, anxious to get active.

"She is and looks like her son wanna ride the little rocket ship outside."

"Ah, man, Rose, she just let her son ride the rocketship by himself and front while she just went into the store like shit's sweet!"

"Pull up over there, but not in front of the store," Symone instructed, already devising her next move, while Pistol pulled up in front of the gym right next to the store. "Stay here, I'll be right back," she ordered, then hopped out of the vehicle and waited in front of the store, determined to be discreet as possible.

"Hey, little man! Are you on your way to the moon?" Symone asked the kid, as if she really cared.

"No, I'm flying to Mars!"

"Okay. When you get there, make sure you have your helmet on."

"I will!" the kid replied, overjoyed.

"Hey, I saw your mommy—Tasha—go into the store."

"Yea, she'll be right back out. She went to get soda."

"Well, can you give her something for me?" she asked, knowing the kid would agree.

"Yes, ma'am."

"Oh, lemme see your hand. Now don't look at it."

"I won't."

"Now, hold it tight."

"I got it!" the kid exclaimed.

"Tell her Symone told you to give her this," she instructed. "Okay, I'll see you later, handsome!" Symone hurried back over the car where Pistol was waiting for her return.

"Rose, what you give little man?" Pistol asked.

"Just a little gift for his mother. Pistol, pull up over there out of sight."

Symone watched as Tasha walked out of the store with two drinks.

"Hey, you ready, little June Bug?" Tasha asked.

"Yea, mommy!"

"What's that you got in your hand, boy?"

"Oh, I forgot, Symone told me to give you this, mommy."

"Who told you to give me what?" Tasha snapped, not wanting to believe what she just heard, especially the name. When her son opened his hand, she saw the bullet. The shock from sight of the bullet caused her to drop both drinks she had in her hands. She snatched her son up and sprinted to her car, where she nervously looked around before getting inside and drove off.

"Rose, why you let her go?" a confused Pistol asked.

"I just wanted her to feel my presence, that's all, because all she's going to feel is slugs real soon. I promise you that. Come on, take me back to Brooklyn."

***

Lorenzo stepped out of his black Range Rover and walked as he conversed with Muscle over the phone.

"Yeah, Tasha told me what happened earlier today," he said into the receiver. "Red Invee going to call me around eleven-thirty tonight before lockdown, then I'ma let her know we going to move forward. Right now I'm picking up my date, so I'ma call you and let you know what she say then."

"Cool. Peace, homie," replied Muscle.

Lorenzo hung up and placed the phone in his top left jacket pocket. He looked at Sony standing in the front lobby of the hotel. Lorenzo stopped to take in her beauty. She was wearing an all-red dress that was hugging her body, accentuating all of her curves. She had an open-toe Red Bottoms. Her fingernails were red. She was wearing a black diamond necklace. Her hair was pressed down to her shoulders. Red lipstick gave her mouth a glowing pout. When Sony spotted, Lorenzo she smiled as she sashayed up to him.

"You look beautiful," he complimented.

"Thank you, so, where are you taking me tonight?" Sony asked.

"I closed down the restaurant tonight just for you, so we can have a private dinner."

"Lorenzo, you didn't have to do all of that."

"Listen, I told you the other night that I'ma treat you like the queen you are." Sony just smiled at Lorenzo's charm.

When they walked into the restaurant, Lorenzo had a table set up for them with candy and a bottle of wine on ice.

"Lorenzo, this is like too much," Sony said in disbelief.

"This just the beginning, I promise you," he shot back.

"Lorenzo, what if I tell you that I don't want dinner? What if I want something else tonight?"

"Like what, sexy?" he asked out of curiosity.

Sony didn't respond. She just walked up to Lorenzo and started kissing him, letting him know exactly what she meant. Lorenzo picked her up as they were in a tongue-at-war session, and placed her on the table. Sony looked into his eyes seductively before laying back on the table. He pushed her dress up and placed her leg upon his shoulders. He kissed her inner thighs slowly as she placed her hands on his head, then she moved her hips until her pussy found his lips. He locked his arms around her legs as he tongued her clit and pressed down on it with smooth, sensual licks. The more he moved his tongue in a circular motion around her pussy walls, the more Sony moaned and shivered. Sony managed to raise herself up, pushing Lorenzo back. She jumped down from the table until she was face to face with Lorenzo. Sony dropped down to her knees and undid his pants until they fell to the floor. She looked up at Lorenzo, as she pulled his boxers down, grabbed his long dick and started licking and sucking the head, rotating both hands on his dick. While she was sucking it, Lorenzo had his eyes closed. He started fucking her mouth, trying desperately to shove every single inch down her throat while she groped his balls as she devoured his cock. Lorenzo pulled back, picked her up and bent her over the table, leaving her dress hiked up. Sony spread her legs apart as Lorenzo inserted his manhood inside of her.

"Um—daddy, pull it out some. It's too thick, daddy!"

"Don't worry—I'ma take it nice and slow, baby," Lorenzo assured her, then wrapped his arms around her stomach and pulled her closer to him. "Damn, baby, you wet as water! I swear this pussy so good!"

"Then make it cum for me, daddy," Sony urged softly.

Lorenzo began pumping harder and harder until he busted all inside of her vagina.

"Damn, bae, I think I just planted a baby in you!" exclaimed an exhausted Lorenzo.

"Shid, you might've, how I felt it in my stomach!" Sony shot back. "Where's the restroom so I can go wash up?" she asked.

"Over there to the left, baby girl." Sony picked up her purse and waltzed to the restroom.

Lorenzo picked up his pants and sat down at the table, waiting for his date to return.

He pulled out his phone and saw that he had a missed call from Muscle. He texted him immediately and told him he was at the restaurant. Lorenzo glanced up and smiled when he saw Sony come back out the bathroom.

"Damn, what took you so long, sexy?" he asked.

"Boy, you know I had to freshen up, especially with all that fuckin cum you just put in me, Mr. Lorenzo!"

"That's small. Just wait till I get you in my house."

"I can't wait!" Sony exclaimed.

Lorenzo poured both of them some wine as they sat and chatted for the next twenty minutes. Muscle pulled up out front, and texted Lorenzo to inform him he was outside. Symone walked from the back of the restaurant, but halted at the kitchen doors and stared at Lorenzo as she pulled her gun out. Lorenzo got up and walked to the bar to get a bottle of Cîroc. He looked back at Sony who was smiling at him when he turned around. Symone had a 9mm aimed at his face. He turned back around and saw Sony still smiling at him.

"What the fuck!" he spat, trying to put the pieces to the puzzle together.

"I'ma ask you one time, who pushed the button against me?" Symone asked sternly.

"Does it matter? Either way, you're a dead bitch!" Lorenzo snapped, not intimidated at all.

"Not before you, pussy!" Lorenzo stared at Symone. Before a blink of an eye, he felt the bullets ripping through him as he fell backwards onto the floor.

Muscle heard the shots and ran inside of the restaurant. Symone spotted him as he was entering. She contemplated firing at him as well.

"Muscle, what's up, baby boy? I'm glad you stopped by so I can kill you also!" Sony stood up and jogged over to Symone's side.

"Hurry up and get to the car around back. I'll meet you outside," Symone ordered.

Symone glanced down at Lorenzo's motionless body once more, and pointed her gun at his head.

Muscle began shooting at her, as she fired one shot into Lorenzo's head and ran out of the back door. Muscle ran up to Lorenzo's near lifeless body. All he could do was stare down at Lorenzo.

"Damn, Lorenzo, how she catch you slippin' like that? Fuck man!" Muscle dropped to his knees and picked Lorenzo's head up gently as blood bubbles came from his mouth. Lorenzo's phone began going off. He tried desperately to retrieve it from inside his pocket, but to no avail. Muscle retrieved it out of his pocket.

"Hello."

"You have a collect call from Jamila LaCross. Press one to accept." Muscle followed the instruction.

"Hello."

"Who is this?" Jamila asked, not recognizing the voice.

"Muscle."

"Where's Lorenzo? And why do you have his phone?"

"Jamila, Symone just whacked him, caught him slippin'," he answered. "Shorty hit him up like five times. Bruh not breathing. Lorenzo, Lorenzo, come on, man, shake through this shit, man! Jamila, you there? Jamila—Jamila—Lorenzo, breathe, man." Lorenzo was lying on his back, bleeding tremendously. His vision was blurry, and his heart was pounding inside of his chest, making it difficult for him to breathe. He was hearing a lot of noise in the background from police sirens and EMT workers yelling. He heard Muscle talking on the phone to someone, as he felt his body being lifted and placed on a flat surface. Lorenzo heard a female voice shouting.

"Get me oxygen, hurry up! Stay with me, Lorenzo. Try to keep your eyes open for me." She paused to issue a command. "Get the doctor on the phone and let him know that a Hispanic man between the age of twenty-eight and thirty-two has been shot four times, two shot to the shoulder, one to the right breast plate, and one that grazed him on the right side of his head. Our ambulance is like four minutes away from the hospital."

Lorenzo took one last breath before he flatlined.

"He's flatlined! He's flatlined!" the lady shouted. "Hurry get me the defibrillator!" she ordered "3-2-1 shock—no response! Again. 3-2-1—we got him back. Stay with me, Lorenzo, we almost there!"

Chapter 55

Joe Scott walked up to Kent Lenacci in the park.

"Hey, Joe, long time no see!" Kent spoke in excitement.

"You're right, it's been too long, Kent," Joe replied. "It's a beautiful day today. Let's take a walk around the lake, shall we?"

"Yeah, it is a good day for a walk, Joe, come on."

"So, tell me, Kent, what is it that you wanted to talk to me about?"

"Word has got back to me that you decided to become allies with Symone Rose."

"You know, Kent," Joe paused for a second, "the old days are gone and it's a new day and time, and let's face the fact—in the streets of NYC, gangs run them. The Mafia don't strike fear in the hearts of people like they used to. People, it seems, only respect violence and money. So, if I have to make allies with a nigga just to keep control of my turf, so be it. I don't mind being in the background making the money, Kent."

"You make a good point, Joe," Kent admitted. "So, what are you going to do about the spark that's about to start the fire between the LaCross family and Rose family?" he questioned. "You know, history will show that Red Invee never lost a war where a lot of great men have failed to defeat her," Kent added.

"You're right, Kent, but what I do know is that Rose is just as ruthless and blood-hungry as Red Invee," Joe stated. "And one thing I do know about Red Invee is, she's not going to the extreme as Rose," he added. "Just look how she got Lorenzo, whom I heard that she shot over six times."

"Yeah, I heard the same thing, Joe," Kent agreed. "They say it was due to Lorenzo having one of her top men shot, which I still don't see how you could even eat at the same table with the same female that hung you upside down out of the twenty-sixth floor window." Kent shook his head in disbelief.

"I think about that a lot also, Kent."

"Lemme ask you this—How could you sit at the table with Tony after he killed your brother?" questioned Kent.

"If you could sit at the table with a man who murdered your mother's child, I know I can sit at a table with a female who took over two of my hole-in-the-wall establishment," Joe stated honestly.

"You make a valid point, Joe. Just be ready because this might be the storm that you're not prepared to walk through." Kent was serious. "Look, Red Invee will be home real soon, Joe, where she has five years to try to make up for. Once she emerges, it's going to be flashes of lights, bullets flying, and puddles of blood left on the ground. As of right now, Rose is the enemy and whomever else that's standing with her against the Queen Don." Kent glanced at Joe, shook his hand and walked back over to where his men were waiting for him to return.

"You ready, boss?" one of Joe's men asked.

"Yeah, let's get out of here."

Joe had ended a battle to start a war that three families couldn't win.

"We'll be dropping a rose over his grave real soon," Kent uttered, then got inside of the car.

Joe watched him as he drove off. "What was that about, boss?" one of Joe's men asked

"Just someone trying to gather up information on where we stood. Come on, let's get out of here," Joe instructed.

Chapter 56

"So, is he dead?" questioned Halo.

"That's what I don't know, Halo," Symone replied. "I shot him literally four times up close, then stood over him and shot him in the head right before Muscle began shooting at me," she added.

"I'll find out. I'll have a few of my friends look into it for me."

"Lemme know, Halo."

Symone sat down at her desk and lit a *black-n-mild*. She didn't know if Lorenzo was dead or alive. Either way, Symone had gotten her point across, but in her eyes, it was: *if you kill my cat, I kill your dog.* Jamila could have Queens because right now Symone was the Don of Brooklyn. And if Red Invee wanted smoke, then she would just be another body being fished out of the Hudson River. Rule number one: *fuck love*; rule number two: *kill or be killed.*

Symone got up and walked to the mirror to look at her reflection before pointing her gun at it, then said to herself: "Killers respect killers," then she put her gun down and had to face the fact that there was no turning back. Either she was going to be standing over Red Invee, or Red Invee was going to be standing over her.

SAYNOMORE

Chapter 57

Masi walked up to Muscle as he was sitting on the hood of his car, smoking a blunt and listening to 50 Cent's 'Many Men'.

"You good, homie?" asked Masi.

"Yeah, I'm good, bro, just can't get over this shit, Masi!"

"It's been four months now, wasn't shit you could've done about it," Masi said.

"I see your point, Masi. We all know how Symone gives it up. She gives no fucks, and Lorenzo was aware what time it was before he had us pull up on shorty sideways at *Passions*."

"Lemme hit your blunt, fam," said Masi. Muscle hopped off his hood and passed Masi the blunt.

"You right, Masi, he shoulda off dat bitch when he had his chance! Then she had Tasha down bad and gave lil' man a bullet, and we all know she don't give a damn about killing no kids!" Masi coughed twice as he passed the blunt back to Muscle.

"Look, Muscle, Red Invee told us to hold shit down till she come home. She only got like five months left. Me, you, Tasha, Crystal, Dro, and twenty others got this. Fuck Symone! If I see that bitch, it's *bang bang* on sight! I got da extended forty-round clip, and every bullet got that bitch's name on it!" Masi spat angrily. "But look, this what I came to tell you—I found where the babymama of one of her soldiers resides."

"Who?" Muscle questioned.

"The white boy, J-Mitch. His BM stay off 45th street," Masi revealed.

"Wuzzup, *bang bang*?" Muscle pulled the blunt and glanced at Masi, then dapped him up.

"*Bang bang*," said Masi.

***

Jamila was lying in her bunk when Ms. Rose walked in her cell. Jamila sat up and looked at Ms. Rose.

"How you feeling?" Ms. Rose asked.

"I'm good, Ms. Rose."

"No, you're not, Jamila, I can see it in your eyes and I can just hear it in your voice."

Jamila let out a sigh to confirm Ms. Rose's intuition before speaking. "You know I just been thinking how I gave her everything and how she just up and turned on me," Jamila stated sadly. "For the past few weeks, I been thinking about killing her and just me hearing Muscle yelling, telling Lorenzo to breathe. Shaking it off just makes me want to give her a real bloody death!" Jamila spat.

"Jamila, you have something that Symone don't have, you have the people's love and respect of the mob. She only has the people's fear. She didn't do what you did for the mob. That's why the families that don't like you still have respect and love for you. As for the ones who turned against you for her, bury them with her. Jamila, you have to make a statement to show you are not to be fucked with, not even by your own family. However, there will be plenty of time for you to get back at your sister. Now, what you need to be doing is thinking about what you're going to do once you leave this place in the next few months."

"Take back what's mine and let NYC know that there is only one Queen and she's back!" Jamila spat. Before she could utter another word, Jamila heard one of the officers calling her name.

"Jamila LaCross, attorney visit!" the officer announced.

Jamila looked at Ms. Rose, turned around and looked at Amber as she was walking in the cell door.

"Why you staring at us, Jamila?" Ms. Rose said. "You the one that has the attorney visit, not us!"

"Let's see what he has to say to me today," Jamila said.

Ms. Rose watched as Jamila walked out of the cell to her attorney's visit.

When Jamila got to her destination, she spotted Mr. Williams seated behind the table, as the officer opened the door for her to enter.

"Hello, Jamila, it's been a while—"

"Yes, it has, Mr. Williams, four years and nine months to be exact," Jamila cut her attorney off. "So tell me, what brings you by today?" she asked out of curiosity.

"I have some good news for you."

"And what's that?"

"You are being teletype, meaning you go home tomorrow," he announced.

"Don't tell me that. Tell me you are not playing, are you?" she asked in disbelief.

"I wouldn't play with you like that—You're going home," he clarified.

Jamila shot to her feet, waltzed around the table and gave Mr. Williams a hug.

"Thank you so much for all you've done for me, thank you!"

"No, Ms. LaCross, thank you for trusting me to get the job done," he replied with a smile.

Jamila turned around and walked back to her cell where she couldn't stop smiling.

"Jamila, why is that smile so bright on your face?" Amber asked.

"Amber, I go home tomorrow," she announced.

"Oh, my God, Jamila, that's wonderful! Who are you going to call to come pick you up?"

"No one, I'll be fine," Jamila answered, still in disbelief.

Jamila looked out of the door at Ms. Rose playing chess. Ms. Rose placed her index finger to her mouth, winked at Jamila, and said: "Congrats, beautiful!"

SAYNOMORE

Chapter 58

Symone was sitting at her desk inside her office conversing with Halo when Lola suddenly waltzed into her office.

"Rose, you need to see this," Lola insisted.

"And what's that?" a curious Symone asked. Lola picked up the remote from the table and turned to the news, where they all saw Jamila walking out of the prison to a black limo where she had Muscle and Masi waiting for her.

"Ms. LaCross, can I ask a question?" Jamila stopped and looked at the reporter.

"Sure, what is your question?"

"Now that you're out of prison after five years, what are you going to do now?"

Jamila stared dead into the camera. "I'm going to Brooklyn to put the trash in the dumpster. Brooklyn's going to be my new home now."

Symone got off her desk and poured everyone a drink.

"Rose, what are we drinking to?" asked Halo.

"A dead bitch!"

The End

SAYNOMORE

Lock Down Publications and Ca$h Presents assisted publishing packages.

BASIC PACKAGE $499
Editing
Cover Design
Formatting

UPGRADED PACKAGE $800
Typing
Editing
Cover Design
Formatting

ADVANCE PACKAGE $1,200
Typing
Editing
Cover Design
Formatting
Copyright registration
Proofreading
Upload book to Amazon

LDP SUPREME PACKAGE $1,500
Typing
Editing
Cover Design
Formatting
Copyright registration
Proofreading
Set up Amazon account
Upload book to Amazon
Advertise on LDP Amazon and Facebook page

***Other services available upon request. Additional charges
may apply
Lock Down Publications
P.O. Box 944
Stockbridge, GA 30281-9998
Phone # 470 303-9761

Submission Guideline

Submit the first three chapters of your completed manuscript to ldpsubmissions@gmail.com, subject line: Your book's title. The manuscript must be in a .doc file and sent as an attachment. Document should be in Times New Roman, double spaced and in size 12 font. Also, provide your synopsis and full contact information. If sending multiple submissions, they must each be in a separate email.

Have a story but no way to send it electronically? You can still submit to LDP/Ca$h Presents. Send in the first three chapters, written or typed, of your completed manuscript to:

LDP: Submissions Dept
Po Box 944
Stockbridge, Ga 30281

DO NOT send original manuscript. Must be a duplicate.

Provide your synopsis and a cover letter containing your full contact information.

Thanks for considering LDP and Ca$h Presents.

<u>NEW RELEASES</u>

AN UNFORESEEN LOVE 2 by MEESHA
KING OF THE TRENCHES by GHOST & TRANAY
ADAMS
A DOPEBOY'S DREAM by ROMELL TUKES
MONEY MAFIA by JIBRIL WILLIAMS
QUEEN OF THE ZOO by BLACK MIGO
MOB TIES 4 by SAYNOMORE

STREET KINGS III

PAID IN BLOOD III

CARTEL KILLAZ IV

DOPE GODS III

Hood Rich

SINS OF A HUSTLA II

ASAD

RICH $AVAGE II

By Troublesome

YAYO V

Bred In The Game 2

S. Allen

CREAM III

By Yolanda Moore

SON OF A DOPE FIEND III

HEAVEN GOT A GHETTO II

By Renta

LOYALTY AIN'T PROMISED III

By Keith Williams

I'M NOTHING WITHOUT HIS LOVE II

SINS OF A THUG II

TO THE THUG I LOVED BEFORE II

By Monet Dragun

QUIET MONEY IV

EXTENDED CLIP III

THUG LIFE IV

By **Trai'Quan**

THE STREETS MADE ME IV

By **Larry D. Wright**

IF YOU CROSS ME ONCE II

By **Anthony Fields**

THE STREETS WILL NEVER CLOSE II

By K'ajji

HARD AND RUTHLESS III

THE BILLIONAIRE BENTLEYS II

Von Diesel

KILLA KOUNTY II

By Khufu

MONEY GAME II

By Smoove Dolla

A GANGSTA'S KARMA II

By FLAME

JACK BOYZ VERSUS DOPE BOYZ

A DOPEBOY'S DREAM III

By Romell Tukes

MURDA WAS THE CASE II

Elijah R. Freeman

THE STREETS NEVER LET GO II

By Robert Baptiste

AN UNFORESEEN LOVE III

By **Meesha**

KING OF THE TRENCHES II
by **GHOST & TRANAY ADAMS**

MONEY MAFIA

By **Jibril Williams**

QUEEN OF THE ZOO II

By **Black Migo**

<u>Available Now</u>

SAYNOMORE

RESTRAINING ORDER **I & II**

By **CA$H & Coffee**

LOVE KNOWS NO BOUNDARIES **I II & III**

By **Coffee**

RAISED AS A GOON I, II, III & IV

BRED BY THE SLUMS I, II, III

BLAST FOR ME I & II

ROTTEN TO THE CORE I II III

A BRONX TALE I, II, III

DUFFLE BAG CARTEL I II III IV V VI

HEARTLESS GOON I II III IV V

A SAVAGE DOPEBOY I II

DRUG LORDS I II III

CUTTHROAT MAFIA I II

KING OF THE TRENCHES

By **Ghost**

LAY IT DOWN **I & II**

LAST OF A DYING BREED I II

BLOOD STAINS OF A SHOTTA I & II III

By **Jamaica**

LOYAL TO THE GAME I II III

LIFE OF SIN I, II III

By **TJ & Jelissa**

BLOODY COMMAS I & II

SKI MASK CARTEL I II & III

KING OF NEW YORK I II,III IV V

RISE TO POWER I II III

COKE KINGS I II III IV

BORN HEARTLESS I II III IV

KING OF THE TRAP I II

By **T.J. Edwards**

IF LOVING HIM IS WRONG…I & II

LOVE ME EVEN WHEN IT HURTS I II III

By **Jelissa**

WHEN THE STREETS CLAP BACK I & II III

THE HEART OF A SAVAGE I II III

MONEY MAFIA

By **Jibril Williams**

A DISTINGUISHED THUG STOLE MY HEART I II & III

LOVE SHOULDN'T HURT I II III IV

RENEGADE BOYS I II III IV

PAID IN KARMA I II III

SAVAGE STORMS I II

AN UNFORESEEN LOVE I II

By **Meesha**

A GANGSTER'S CODE I &, II III

A GANGSTER'S SYN I II III

THE SAVAGE LIFE I II III

CHAINED TO THE STREETS I II III

BLOOD ON THE MONEY I II III

By J-Blunt

PUSH IT TO THE LIMIT

By **Bre' Hayes**

BLOOD OF A BOSS **I, II, III, IV, V**

SHADOWS OF THE GAME

TRAP BASTARD

By **Askari**

THE STREETS BLEED MURDER **I, II & III**

THE HEART OF A GANGSTA I II& III

By **Jerry Jackson**

SAYNOMORE

CUM FOR ME I II III IV V VI VII

An **LDP Erotica Collaboration**

BRIDE OF A HUSTLA **I II & II**

THE FETTI GIRLS **I, II& III**

CORRUPTED BY A GANGSTA I, II III, IV

BLINDED BY HIS LOVE

THE PRICE YOU PAY FOR LOVE I, II ,III

DOPE GIRL MAGIC I II III

By **Destiny Skai**

WHEN A GOOD GIRL GOES BAD

By **Adrienne**

THE COST OF LOYALTY I II III

By Kweli

A GANGSTER'S REVENGE **I II III & IV**

THE BOSS MAN'S DAUGHTERS I II III IV V

A SAVAGE LOVE **I & II**

BAE BELONGS TO ME I II

A HUSTLER'S DECEIT I, II, III

WHAT BAD BITCHES DO I, II, III

SOUL OF A MONSTER I II III

KILL ZONE

A DOPE BOY'S QUEEN I II III

By **Aryanna**

A KINGPIN'S AMBITON

A KINGPIN'S AMBITION **II**

I MURDER FOR THE DOUGH

By **Ambitious**

TRUE SAVAGE I II III IV V VI VII

DOPE BOY MAGIC I, II, III

MIDNIGHT CARTEL I II III

CITY OF KINGZ I II
NIGHTMARE ON SILENT AVE
By **Chris Green**
A DOPEBOY'S PRAYER
By **Eddie "Wolf" Lee**
THE KING CARTEL **I, II & III**
By **Frank Gresham**
THESE NIGGAS AIN'T LOYAL **I, II & III**
By **Nikki Tee**
GANGSTA SHYT **I II &III**
By **CATO**
THE ULTIMATE BETRAYAL
By **Phoenix**
BOSS'N UP **I , II & III**
By **Royal Nicole**
I LOVE YOU TO DEATH
By **Destiny J**
I RIDE FOR MY HITTA
I STILL RIDE FOR MY HITTA
By **Misty Holt**
LOVE & CHASIN' PAPER
By **Qay Crockett**
TO DIE IN VAIN
SINS OF A HUSTLA
By **ASAD**
BROOKLYN HUSTLAZ
By **Boogsy Morina**
BROOKLYN ON LOCK I & II
By **Sonovia**
GANGSTA CITY

SAYNOMORE

By **Teddy Duke**
A DRUG KING AND HIS DIAMOND I & II III
A DOPEMAN'S RICHES
HER MAN, MINE'S TOO I, II
CASH MONEY HO'S
THE WIFEY I USED TO BE I II
By **Nicole Goosby**
TRAPHOUSE KING **I II & III**
KINGPIN KILLAZ I II III
STREET KINGS I II
PAID IN BLOOD **I II**
CARTEL KILLAZ I II III
DOPE GODS I II
By **Hood Rich**
LIPSTICK KILLAH **I, II, III**
CRIME OF PASSION I II & III
FRIEND OR FOE I II III
By **Mimi**
STEADY MOBBN' **I, II, III**
THE STREETS STAINED MY SOUL I II
By **Marcellus Allen**
WHO SHOT YA **I, II, III**
SON OF A DOPE FIEND I II
HEAVEN GOT A GHETTO
Renta
GORILLAZ IN THE BAY **I II III IV**
TEARS OF A GANGSTA I II
3X KRAZY I II
DE'KARI
TRIGGADALE I II III

MURDAROBER WAS THE CASE

Elijah R. Freeman

GOD BLESS THE TRAPPERS I, II, III

THESE SCANDALOUS STREETS I, II, III

FEAR MY GANGSTA I, II, III IV, V

THESE STREETS DON'T LOVE NOBODY I, II

BURY ME A G I, II, III, IV, V

A GANGSTA'S EMPIRE I, II, III, IV

THE DOPEMAN'S BODYGAURD I II

THE REALEST KILLAZ I II III

THE LAST OF THE OGS I II III

Tranay Adams

THE STREETS ARE CALLING

Duquie Wilson

MARRIED TO A BOSS I II III

By Destiny Skai & Chris Green

KINGZ OF THE GAME I II III IV V

Playa Ray

SLAUGHTER GANG I II III

RUTHLESS HEART I II III

By Willie Slaughter

FUK SHYT

By Blakk Diamond

DON'T F#CK WITH MY HEART I II

By Linnea

ADDICTED TO THE DRAMA I II III

IN THE ARM OF HIS BOSS II

By Jamila

YAYO I II III IV

A SHOOTER'S AMBITION I II

SAYNOMORE

BRED IN THE GAME

By S. Allen

TRAP GOD I II III

RICH $AVAGE

By Troublesome

FOREVER GANGSTA

GLOCKS ON SATIN SHEETS I II

By Adrian Dulan

TOE TAGZ I II III

LEVELS TO THIS SHYT I II

By Ah'Million

KINGPIN DREAMS I II III

By Paper Boi Rari

CONFESSIONS OF A GANGSTA I II III IV

By Nicholas Lock

I'M NOTHING WITHOUT HIS LOVE

SINS OF A THUG

TO THE THUG I LOVED BEFORE

By Monet Dragun

CAUGHT UP IN THE LIFE I II III

THE STREETS NEVER LET GO

By Robert Baptiste

NEW TO THE GAME I II III

MONEY, MURDER & MEMORIES I II III

By **Malik D. Rice**

LIFE OF A SAVAGE I II III

A GANGSTA'S QUR'AN I II III

MURDA SEASON I II III

GANGLAND CARTEL I II III

CHI'RAQ GANGSTAS I II III

KILLERS ON ELM STREET I II III
JACK BOYZ N DA BRONX I II III
A DOPEBOY'S DREAM I II
By **Romell Tukes**
LOYALTY AIN'T PROMISED I II
By Keith Williams
QUIET MONEY I II III
THUG LIFE I II III
EXTENDED CLIP I II
By **Trai'Quan**
THE STREETS MADE ME I II III
By **Larry D. Wright**
THE ULTIMATE SACRIFICE I, II, III, IV, V, VI
KHADIFI
IF YOU CROSS ME ONCE
ANGEL I II
IN THE BLINK OF AN EYE
By **Anthony Fields**
THE LIFE OF A HOOD STAR
By Ca$h & Rashia Wilson
THE STREETS WILL NEVER CLOSE
By K'ajji
CREAM I II
By Yolanda Moore
NIGHTMARES OF A HUSTLA I II III
By King Dream
CONCRETE KILLA I II
By Kingpen
HARD AND RUTHLESS I II
MOB TOWN 251

SAYNOMORE

THE BILLIONAIRE BENTLEYS
By Von Diesel
GHOST MOB
Stilloan Robinson
MOB TIES I II III IV
By SayNoMore
BODYMORE MURDERLAND I II III
By Delmont Player
FOR THE LOVE OF A BOSS
By C. D. Blue
MOBBED UP I II III IV
By King Rio
KILLA KOUNTY
By Khufu
MONEY GAME
By Smoove Dolla
A GANGSTA'S KARMA
By FLAME
KING OF THE TRENCHES II
by **GHOST & TRANAY ADAMS**
QUEEN OF THE ZOO
By **Black Migo**

BOOKS BY LDP'S CEO, CA$H

TRUST IN NO MAN

TRUST IN NO MAN 2

TRUST IN NO MAN 3

BONDED BY BLOOD

SHORTY GOT A THUG

THUGS CRY

THUGS CRY 2

THUGS CRY 3

TRUST NO BITCH

TRUST NO BITCH 2

TRUST NO BITCH 3

TIL MY CASKET DROPS

RESTRAINING ORDER

RESTRAINING ORDER 2

IN LOVE WITH A CONVICT

LIFE OF A HOOD STAR

SAYNOMORE